Allison

Special Merit Award to The O'Brien Press

READING ASSOCIATION OF IRELAND

'for exceptional care, skill and professionalism in publishing, resulting in a consistently high standard in all of the children's books published by The O'Brien Press'

Tatiana Strelkoff

Tatiana was born in Iowa, USA, into a family of Russian background. Later she studied anthropology at UCLA, then went to Italy where she met her Italian husband. She now lives in Rome where she writes subtitles for major Italian films, including *The Star Man* by Giuseppe Tornatore, and Ettore Scola's film *The Story of a Poor Young Man*; she has also translated screenplays. Her first book, *The Changer*, is a children's book.

This book grew out of Tatiana's own experience. She discovered that a much-loved friend had hidden the fact that she was gay all through their teenage years for fear of the effect this would have on her friendships and on her relationship with her family. Tatiana was shocked that someone so close to her would go unsupported through the pain of this kind of secrecy, and she wrote this story about a young girl's discovery of her 'different' sexuality in the hope of fostering understanding and tolerance.

Allison

TATIANA STRELKOFF

THE O'BRIEN PRESS
DUBLIN

First published 1998 by The O'Brien Press Ltd.,
20 Victoria Road, Rathgar, Dublin 6, Ireland.
Tel. +353 1 4923333 Fax. +353 1 4922777
e-mail: books@obrien.ie
http://www.obrien.ie

ISBN: 0-86278-559-6

British Library Cataloguing-in-publication Data
Allison : girl meets girl - a story of first love
1.Lesbians - Fictions
2.Young adult fiction
I:Title
823.9'14[J]

1 2 3 4 5 6 7 8 9 10
97 98 99 00 01 02 03 04 05

The O'Brien Press receives
assistance from

The Arts Council
An Chomhairle Ealaíon

The characters in this book are fictional and bear no resemblance to any persons living or dead. If any such resemblance occurs it is entirely accidental and is not the intention of the author.

Typesetting, layout, design: The O'Brien Press Ltd.
Cover illustration: Angela Clarke
Cover separations: Lithoset Ltd., Dublin
Printing: Cox & Wyman Ltd.

For Lyena

1

KAREN HAD BEEN IN TENSINGTON for exactly two months, if she counted the weekend trip with her mother to size the city up. It was long enough to meet the neighbours, start school and fall in love. Despite the neighbours' aloofness and the school's newness, it was the falling in love that was causing the most trouble. That's why Karen tried so hard to call it something else – admiration, infatuation – but the words fought their way to her lips and refused to succumb to her mental acrobatics. No, she was definitely *in love*. In love with Allison. And nobody must know.

Karen paced the length of the room, her hands in her jeans pockets. That was the problem with growing up too fast, she brooded. She knew herself too well and had enough experience to name things as they were. Not to mention that Allison was not an easy person to hide. She was like a beacon, her red hair gloriously illuminating her presence. When she was with her, Karen felt Allison's radiance spotlight her as well. She could imagine people wondering what in the world Allison saw in that shy new girl with the mousy brown hair. Certainly she couldn't be anyone special.

How often since they'd met had Karen gone to the mirror as she did now, to stare at her reflection? Be objective, she told herself, she was ordinary. Her brown hair was simply brown. No blond highlights or chestnut undertones. Just brown, parted in the middle and gathered in a fat pony-tail that reached the small of her back. Her eyes, too. Brown. She had an olive complexion that went plain brown in the summer, causing her brother Danny to nickname her 'Coconut', which she barely tolerated.

She couldn't get over how she was just as tall as Allison and weighed the same but looked so different. Allison's body rose and curved precisely the way a woman's body should, while Karen's remained stubbornly unflattering. No breasts, no waist. Yet something in this entirely unaffecting image had attracted Allison. It was she who had made the first move. Karen could still remember every word.

It had happened in the locker room.

'You're new,' Allison had said, slamming her locker shut. 'These old things are touchy. Let me show you.'

She put her hand on Karen's and moved Karen's fingers aside in a gesture that was something between a caress and a motherly reprimand. 'You have to know how to handle them.'

Then she looked at Karen with blue eyes that made Karen think of Mediterranean water. 'What's the combination?'

'Oh, I wrote it down,' Karen stuttered, surprised at her own reaction. 'I know it, I just can't get it open.' She fumbled in her schoolbag and pulled out a slip of paper. 'Twenty-seven, thirteen, thirty-four.'

Allison tapped the lock a few times at each number and, before opening it, tapped it again a little harder. The locker swung open on its own. 'It's easy once you get the hang of it.' Allison stood back and smiled. 'You got plans for lunch?'

They both had packed lunches and ate on the grassy hill in front of the school, the autumn sun warming their backs. Allison chatted away amiably, giving Karen a run-down of what was what at Seaworth High.

By the time lunch was over Karen knew more about her new high school than she cared to. She gathered from the frequent interruptions by other kids that Allison was popular, but Allison never mentioned any boyfriends. She learned that Allison's mother was a poet and that her father was a journalist for the city paper, but Allison said she was close to failing English and didn't follow politics.

Karen was entranced by Allison, and found herself looking away in embarrassment whenever Allison caught her eye. Without understanding why, Karen was afraid of what Allison might see there.

'I'm glad we met,' Allison said when the bell rang. She stood up and put her hand on Karen's arm. 'I hope we can be friends.' She slung her bag over her shoulder and walked up the concrete steps to the building.

If they hadn't had lockers next to each other Karen would never have had the courage to speak to her again, but as it was they saw each other every hour, practically, and becoming friends was easy. What came after that was not.

'Could you give me a hand?' yelled Karen's mother from the back door.

Karen jumped and turned hastily away from the mirror, already muttering something inane about a speck of dust in her eye. But her mother was busy and Karen realised there'd be no need for explanations. She glanced at her reflection once more before walking down the hall and into the kitchen.

'God, I hate groceries,' Mom groaned as she struggled through the back door clutching three bulging bags against her body. She heaved them onto the kitchen table and kissed Karen on the cheek. 'Start unloading, there's more.'

Methodically, Karen began emptying the grocery bags into separate piles – frozen food first, then fridge, pantry, according to each item.

'Finally!' Mom said, plopping herself dramatically into a kitchen chair. She kicked off her shoes. 'I hate heels, I hate nylons, I hate shopping!' She glanced around the room. 'Is Danny home yet?'

Karen shook her head. 'Today's basketball practice.'

Instantly, her mother hiked up her skirt and swiftly pulled off her tights. 'I wish I felt okay about wearing trousers to work, but I just can't. Grandma won't allow it!'

Karen smiled. Her grandmother had been dead for several years but the powerful woman lived on in their lives, her likes and dislikes and petty prejudices firmly ingrained in the family psyche. It was an inside joke. If you agreed with something rationally but couldn't make the final leap to actually doing it, Grandma's influence was to blame. It explained everything from Mom's unwillingness to wear pants to work to her refusal to accept alimony when she finally divorced Karen and Danny's father and was practically penniless.

That had been only seven years ago, and it had been a long haul since then. Karen still remembered the time when groceries consisted of dried beans, lentils and peas. Still, they'd made it, and the move to Tensington had been the crowning glory – a new and important position for Mom in a well-known advertising firm. Though it meant changing schools right before her senior year, and Danny had to start his freshman year in a new place, Karen came gladly. She felt she'd outgrown the small town of Richmond long before.

'Do you suppose it's storming like this back home?' Mom wondered out loud, as she opened a packet of crackers.

'We are home, Mom,' said Karen, a bit impatiently. 'With all the bad things that happened there I don't understand how you keep missing that place.'

Her mother shrugged. 'Not everything was bad. There were some good years. I had you ... and Danny.'

'Well, we're much better off here.' Karen spilled the apples into the fruit bin. 'I don't miss Richmond a bit.'

Mom looked at her searchingly. 'It's true. You've burned that bridge completely. You won't even talk to Andrew when he calls.'

'He wasn't ever that important,' said Karen lightly, though her words shamed her a little. 'Puppy love,' she added.

'You went steady for two years. I always imagined he was your ... first?'

Karen looked up, startled. She couldn't believe her mother was bringing up a subject she'd always avoided. In fact, one glance was enough to show how hard Mom was trying. Though she was smiling, the rest of her body was tense and straight, her hands actually balled into fists in her lap.

Karen felt a wave of love and pity. Mom wanted so much for them to have the open kind of relationship one reads about in books. It was just that Grandma made it tough, as did the lasting taboos imposed from the very beginning by Karen's father. Karen went to her and hugged her.

'I'm still too young for that,' she lied. 'When the big day comes I'll let you know.'

Karen could feel her mother's body relax. 'I love you, sweetie,' Mom said. 'I hope you'll always come and talk to me.'

Karen nodded but couldn't meet her mother's eyes. How could she talk to someone who was fighting so visibly to stay calm? It was almost scary.

'I've got lots more important things on my mind,' Karen said cheerily, going back to the groceries.

'Oh, yes, darling, I'm sure you do, what with a new school, new friends, new boys ...'

Allison's flaming hair and brilliant smile appeared before Karen's eyes. 'That's it,' she said to her mother.

2

AT FIRST, KAREN SOUGHT ALLISON'S COMPANY GREEDILY. It had been an easy way into the social life at Seaworth. Allison was invited to the football parties, drama class openings and poetry readings. She had friends from all the cliques and seemed perfectly happy to let Karen tag along. Though not quite as outgoing as Allison, Karen was not shy and soon she, too, was making friends of her own. But even when dancing at school discos or gossiping with the band leader, Allison wasn't ever far from Karen's sight. Karen could sense her presence behind her, and she too always had one ear tuned to Allison's conversations – though she'd look away guiltily if Allison caught her watching, Allison always smiled grandly in return. And invariably at some point they would end up together, talking comfortably about whatever was on their minds.

Allison never seemed to grow tired of Karen's company, never betrayed the slightest worry that their friendship was anything out of the ordinary, but as the days progressed Karen grew increasingly aware of how deeply Allison affected her. When she saw her from a distance her heart skipped. Her palms were often sweaty when they talked and, more than once, she caught herself inhaling Allison's perfume like a drug.

Her feelings scared her, partly because they confused her and partly because she was terrified of somehow giving herself away and losing Allison forever. Karen began to watch herself, control her gestures, restrain her impulse to touch Allison's arm or brush away her hair. She forced herself to mingle with boys she didn't care for, looking among them for those who were neither boring nor aggressive. And, very carefully, she began to sound out Allison.

'Roger Dunlap's been watching you all night,' Karen once said as they sipped cokes in the auditorium. Boys were a topic they rarely broached and Karen felt she was walking on thin ice.

Allison glanced over in his direction. 'Romeo and Juliet must have gotten to him,' she said indifferently. 'They staged a great one this year.'

'He seems too shy to come and talk to you.'

Allison nodded. 'Yeah, but he's all right.'

Roger bounded over to where they sat. 'The usual gang

is getting together. You two want a ride over to Joe's?'

'I'm kinda tired,' said Allison, shaking her head. 'Karen'll go.' She turned to walk away. 'See you tomorrow.'

'Allison, wait ...' Karen was unprepared for this.

'We're parked out back,' Roger said, taking Karen's arm.

'No, I ...'

Allison was already at the auditorium doors.

'Allison! Wait!' Karen yelled, trying to push past him. She found herself face-to-face with Joe.

'Want a lift to the party?' he asked.

'No, Joe, thanks. I ... another time,' she said hastily, working her way around him as she spoke.

By the time Karen managed to burst through the big double doors of the auditorium, she could just make out Allison at the bottom of the school steps.

'Allison! Wait! What's the matter?' Karen bounded down the steps, the late November chill bringing tears to her eyes.

Allison stopped and turned around. By the light of a street lamp, Karen could see that her usually happy face looked sad – hurt, almost.

'Are you okay? Why did you leave like that? What's the matter?' Karen was shaking as the cold penetrated her sweater. She'd left her jacket in the auditorium.

Allison looked her square in the eyes. 'Why are you trying to palm Roger Dunlap off on me?'

Karen was speechless.

'If you like him you should have the decency to speak to him yourself, without using me.'

'I ... I don't like him,' Karen stuttered. 'I wasn't trying to use you.'

'What then? What were you trying to do?'

'Nothing. I mean ... he just seemed ...'

'I thought we were friends. We always had so many other things to talk about. If I wanted to talk about guys, or have somebody play match-maker, I would've gone with Charlene, or Gail or Angela ...'

'We *are* friends.' Karen reached out and took Allison's arm. Her stomach contracted sharply. 'I just ... it's that ...' she struggled for the words. 'It's just that you're always with me and I worry sometimes that you might want to be with somebody else.'

Allison's stern gaze softened. 'You silly goose.' She took Karen's hand from her shoulder and held it for an instant before letting go. 'If I wanted to be with some guy I'd tell you.'

Karen looked at the ground. 'We never talk about it, though, and it's ... confusing.'

'Let's go back and get your jacket. You're freezing to death.' Allison started back up the steps with Karen following.

Newly bundled up and out on the street once more, Karen and Allison walked home slowly.

'I've never been big on boys,' Allison said, as she walked on and off the curb alongside Karen. 'I don't hate them or anything, and I have some boys as friends, but I've never wanted to do more, you know what I mean?'

Karen nodded, her hands deep in her jacket pockets, still trembling but more now from the emotion than the cold.

'You hit high school and nobody talks about anything except liking this guy, kissing that one, going all the way. I don't know why, but it just never interested me. Oh, I tried it a few times. Kissing, anyway. Everybody seemed to think it was so great, but it annoyed me. The kiss was always meant to be the start of more. There you'd be, trying to see what a kiss is like, and he'd already be touching your boobs or pressing against your pelvis ...'

Karen nodded. 'Andrew was like that.' She'd never told Allison about Andrew, but Allison guessed.

'A boy in Richmond?'

'I met him my sophomore year and we went steady until I moved. He was nice, actually. I liked him. Funny and sweet in a loopy kind of way, but those kisses always had to lead to all the rest, if not right then, then the minute we could manage it.'

'Did you like it?' Allison had stopped at an intersection. It was eerily quiet for a Saturday night.

Karen took a deep breath. 'It wasn't awful.'

Allison raised her eyebrows.

'It was okay, really.' Karen was ashamed she'd never had the courage to tell Andrew she didn't enjoy it. 'He was gentle and never hurt me and ...'

'And you didn't like it.'

'It's not that I didn't like it!' Karen could feel herself getting angry. 'I thought maybe I had to do it for a while before it felt like much. Besides, it made him happy. What's wrong with making someone you like happy?'

'Nothing,' Allison said. She crossed the street and continued down the right side towards her house.

'I was afraid,' Karen said, catching up with her and taking her arm to stop her. 'I was scared he'd think I was weird.'

Allison patted her arm in that motherly way of hers and started down the street again. 'He would have. Most guys do. Girls, too, but they get over it.'

'Nobody seems to think that about you.'

They'd reached Allison's house. Allison stood on the bottom step and looked at Karen. She seemed to tower over her, the light from the house illuminating her from the back and giving her red hair a phosphorescent glow.

'You just don't know the people who do. Gable Cross in physics calls me a dyke, and Phyllis Walkers won't be seen anywhere near me.'

'But so many people like you. You're so popular.'

'One day I talked to my mom about it, the day after a party when Gable tried to push himself on me in the kitchen and I fought him off with a packet of plastic plates. She said I shouldn't worry about being different. She said I should just be exactly the woman I am, that good friends will stay and those who don't were never friends.'

'You told your *mother* about what Gable tried to do!'

'Yes, I know. I'm lucky. Most kids can't talk to their parents like I can. And Mom has a way of making my biggest worries seem funny. She said she knows I'm a perfectly normal girl and that I should just enjoy growing up.'

'Are you ... gay, then?' Again, Karen could not meet Allison's eyes.

Allison stepped down to the street. 'I don't really know what I am. I just try to take Mom's advice and not worry about it. I try to have fun with friends, pass that damn English exam and fill out college application forms. Maybe one day I'll find out.'

'Meet Prince Charming ...' Karen offered.

Allison laughed. 'Ah, yes, the right man to set this frozen heart on fire ...' She looked serious suddenly. 'Maybe sex is not for me. It's crossed my mind.'

'You mean ever?'

Allison shrugged. 'We'll see, I guess. Sometimes I imagine kissing someone, and having it be sweet and tender and enough ... all on its own.'

'Someone like ...' Karen willed herself to look into Allison's face.

Allison smiled her radiant smile. 'You.' She reached out

to Karen's face and kissed her once, swiftly, on the cheek. Then she turned and ran up the steps to her house.

Before Karen could react, Allison had opened the door and stepped inside.

'See you tomorrow, silly goose!' she yelled before shutting the door.

3

'WHAT WOULD YOU LIKE FOR DINNER?' Karen's mother asked, looking peaceful and relaxed in her blue robe and furry slippers.

'Anything'll be fine, Mom,' Karen said, her head inside the pantry as she put away the grocery bags that were still intact.

Mom opened the refrigerator and surveyed its contents. 'Danny's always ravenous after practice. I think I'll do pork chops and mashed potatoes. Is it you or Dan who doesn't like brussels sprouts?'

'Dan.' Karen pulled several potatoes out of the bag and began peeling them at the sink. Cooking supper with her mother was customary since Grandma died and it usually gave Karen a respite from her troubling thoughts.

'Green salad, then, with everything in it. You know,

you're right, Karen.' Mom came up behind her. 'Things were pretty bad there for a while but look at us now. A full refrigerator, our choice of food, this nice house I rent ... my job.' She gestured at the warmly lit kitchen. 'Maybe in a few years we'll even be able to buy a house of our own. I really couldn't be happier.'

Karen turned partially away from the sink and smiled at her. No matter what happened, Karen knew she would never do anything to rob her mother of this hard-won happiness. Even if it meant white lies and minor humiliations, like her date that night.

'Where's Craig taking you tonight?' asked her mother, as if reading her mind.

Karen turned back quickly to the sink. 'The ice rink, I think. And he's not taking me, Mom. We're going together.'

'Right, sorry, I've been out of the dating scene for a while.'

'Sorry, I didn't mean to snap.'

'He's nice enough, isn't he, Karen? Craig, I mean. You always seem a little ... tense when you two go out.'

Karen didn't have to turn around to see her mother's awkwardness. She could hear it in her voice.

'Sure, Mom. He's a nice guy. Maybe I'm just a little tired. Mid-term finals are in a few weeks and I'm sort of stressed out.'

'You'll do fine, don't you worry. You're a good student and a good girl. Everything a mother could hope for.' She hugged Karen from behind and then began fiddling with the pork chops and the spice rack.

For an instant, a wave of exhaustion washed over Karen's body, forcing her to drop a potato back into the sink and lay the peeler on the counter. She wanted to sit down but fought to remain standing at the sink until the feeling passed.

'Hi, everybody.' Danny walked into the kitchen and threw his lanky body into a kitchen chair. 'What's for dinner?'

'Pork chops and mashed potatoes,' Mom answered from thc stove. 'Sound okay to you?'

'Brilliant,' Danny said, bending down to untie the laces of his high-tops.

Karen heard the catch in Mom's breathing and saw the red flush which started at the base of her neck. Though Mom did not turn away from the stove, Karen knew exactly what her face looked like. Anger rose inside her. She turned on her brother and said sarcastically, 'One week with Dad and you're full-blooded Irish, huh? In your home town people say "great", not "brilliant,"' she added, after Danny looked up at her in puzzlement.

'What's buggin' her?' Danny looked at Mom's back, pointedly ignoring Karen.

Before turning around, Mom collected herself and by the time she had faced Danny, her features were composed. She shrugged. 'It's just odd, that's all, hearing you use Dad's expressions. You never did before.'

Danny shrugged. 'Dad says I'm a lot like he was at my age. We're two good fellas. Dad's great crack to be with.'

Karen snorted. She couldn't help it. Their father had never been able to spend more than five days at a stretch with them before leaving for another job, and yet in the short periods of time he was home he would insist that he was the head of the family, obliging Mom to defer all decision-making to him despite the fact that she ran the household single-handedly ninety-nine percent of the time.

'You and Dad probably didn't spend more than twenty-four hours together that whole week you were there,' Karen shot at her brother. 'If he isn't actually on a job he's on the phone training people long-distance.'

Danny leaned back against the chair and looked at Karen disparagingly. Again Karen heard, more than saw, her mother wince. It was exactly the look Dad was an expert in delivering, and it was deadly. 'Dad can't help it if he's an expert,' Danny said, pronouncing each word carefully as though talking to a child. 'There are very few men who do underwater construction and nobody does it as good as Dad.' The pride in his voice was unmistakable. 'All those years on the North Sea oil rigs had to amount to something. Dad can talk others through any situation, even from a thousand miles away.'

'Dad's just a lowly construction worker in a wet-suit –' Karen began heatedly, steaming from the belittling look Danny had perfected so effortlessly.

'There's no reason to argue about your father's skill,' Mom interrupted, her voice studied and calm. 'He is doubtless one of the few people around who can drive concrete pilings under the ocean and his expertise is very valuable. The fact is simply that you only lived in Ireland a total of five years, Danny. I'm sure you don't even remember Dublin. That's why it's strange to hear you using Irish expressions.'

'It's not a crime,' Danny said nonchalantly, taking his sneakers off by stepping down on the heels. 'Me and Dad spent a lot of time together.' He looked significantly over at Karen. 'I can't help it if the way he talks rubbed off on me. I'm going to wash,' he said as he stood, kicking his shoes casually under the table.

Karen practically jumped from the sink to the door of the kitchen, blocking his path. 'Who's going to take those smelly things out of here?' she demanded, pointing to his shoes.

Danny walked right up to her. Though he was three years younger he was a good two inches taller and, at five feet seven, could easily have been mistaken for an older brother. 'Don't worry. I'll get them later.' He waved Karen aside and walked into the hallway. 'Maybe we ought to get help,' he called from the bathroom doorway. 'Dad's got a terrific Filipino maid. He doesn't even have to brush his own teeth!'

His parting laughter grated on Karen's nerves so badly

she whirled around and took it all out on her mother. 'Why do you let him get away with that? He practically treats *you* like a maid! I thought you weren't going to take that kind of thing anymore!'

The hurt in her mother's eyes made Karen feel instantly guilty. Though Danny's attitude incensed her, she knew that their mother was doing the best she knew how. She had always been a capable, efficient woman, able to take care of her children and run their home cheerfully and lovingly despite her husband's lengthy absences. She'd been an ace plumber, a self-taught electrician, she even managed basic automobile maintenance with aplomb. But whenever their father was home she'd suddenly had to act inept, incapable, uncertain. As a child Karen never noticed, but by the time they had moved to the United States when Karen was ten, the efforts her mother exerted to defer to her husband began to annoy her. And it was probably because her mother was back on her home soil, in touch once more with old friends, living in the same town as her own mother, that she kept getting stronger, and the show of need when their father was home looked to Karen more and more like the play-acting it was.

Dad seemed to sense that, too. His dominance increased proportionately with the length of time he'd been away. Soon he didn't even want their mother to make minor household purchases without consulting him first. He said it was because he needed to keep track of the family budget –

but it had been the last straw. Mom had been balancing their finances throughout their marriage, seeing to all their needs and never once asking for help or a penny more than the allowance allocated by their father. That same week she went out and got a job. The beginning of the end it had been, with fights and tirades and Dad practically accusing her of abandoning her children. But Mom did not relent. In fact, she went that one step further. She filed for divorce.

'It's just a phase, Karen,' her mother was saying, turning back to the stove. 'Lots of boys go through a difficult adolescence. And I'm sure it's harder for Danny, not having his father home.'

'I think it's more than that.' Karen, too, had turned back to the potatoes, her anger ebbing away with the memory of those first few days after her mother had initiated divorce proceedings. Dad had been literally speechless. Karen was thirteen then, and it was clear to her that he simply couldn't believe that her mother meant it. He looked dazed at first, almost humbled. He wasn't actually bad, Karen began to realise then. He simply knew no other way. He was the man and her mother was the woman, and he couldn't believe she wanted it to be different. And Karen knew that, deep-down, he loved them all.

The shock-induced calm was brief. When Mom's lawyer called Dad a week later, all his wounded pride had balled into anger and he was intractable. He railed at the legal system, at the loose morals of American society and, especially, at his own wife's 'questionable integrity'. He fought for custody of the children in court but his job precluded the possibility of being given it. He simply wasn't in one place long enough to call any city home.

'It hasn't been any different really, since the divorce,' Karen said aloud, still peeling potatoes. 'Danny never had Dad home before and he doesn't now. We still spend Christmas day together and Easter. We visit. He calls. Just like before.'

'Danny wasn't fourteen before.' Mom had come over to stand next to Karen. 'Girls seem to have an easier time in their teenage years. Danny is trying to establish his independence, especially being the only boy in the family. He's working on his identity.'

Karen looked over at her and made a face. 'Did you read that in some book?'

Mom reddened. 'Just comparing notes with colleagues,' she said off-handedly. 'I'm not the only one with these problems. We'll manage just the same. Won't we?'

Karen put down the potato peeler and hugged Mom tightly. 'Sure we will,' she said, patting her back. 'We always have.'

'So. We going to eat or what?'

Danny's surprise entrance startled them both and they inadvertently leaped away from each other as if caught in some unacceptable act. 'Give us half an hour,' Mom said cheerfully, patting his shoulder as she went back to the stove. 'I'll call you.'

'Okay. I'll be watching TV,' he said, and walked out of the kitchen slowly, leaving its warmly lit, good-smelling cosiness behind him.

Dinner was tense, and only their mother's heroic efforts at normal conversation kept the atmosphere from total gloom. Danny wasn't the only one with identity problems, Karen thought morosely, trying to combat a persistent light-headedness with extra helpings of potatoes. She had her own problems, compounded that evening with a faintness which refused to go away. It seemed to blur her vision slightly as she dressed for her date and she wondered fleetingly as she went to answer the doorbell whether she might have a brain tumour, just to top things off.

'Ready?' Craig asked, smiling widely, his black skates thrown over his shoulder. His red ski sweater contrasted handsomely with his dark skin and his white-toothed smile was commercially perfect. Nothing from his Irish mother was to be found in his handsome, Hispanic face, but it was precisely her influence that had brought Craig and Karen together in the first place.

'Come in for a sec,' Karen invited him, bowing to Grandma's belief that all friends, boys and girls, should meet the rest of the family.

Craig dropped his skates by the front door before going into the living room. His faded jeans were snug and his dark hair was held in a short pony-tail that rested on the nape of his neck. He was doubtless one of the best-looking guys at Seaworth, someone in whose company Karen could combat the gossip-mongers who were beginning to look with more than just a little interest at the amount of time Karen spent with Allison. Lucky for her, he was also an intelligent person with a crazy sense of humour, which he attributed to his mix-and-match, Mexican-Irish family.

'Hello, Craig,' said Mom, putting her magazine down and getting up from the couch to greet him.

'Mrs Dolan,' Craig said, nodding his head.

'Yo, Gringo!' yelled Danny from the armchair.

'Only this half,' Craig replied, one arm waving wildly and the other hanging limply at his side.

One thing Karen appreciated about Craig was that he didn't get embarrassed easily.

'Don't be too late,' Mom said as she walked them to the door.

'Don't worry, Mrs Dolan. All of us have finals coming up,' Craig said reassuringly, taking Karen's hand.

Karen let him hold it until her mother shut the door. Then she slipped her hand away and jogged over to the passenger side of his blue Toyota.

'Who's Tawni coming with?' Karen asked him as he slid behind the wheel.

'We all prefer it when she comes with her sister but, unfortunately, Jody's still sick with the mumps. It'll probably be someone from the team ... Robbie, or Terry ...'

Craig looked over as Karen slumped in her seat. 'Maybe Lawrence,' he said encouragingly.

Tears were forming in Karen's eyes and she blinked them away.

'Don't tell me you're not up to it,' Craig pleaded. 'It's been two weeks since Tawni and I ...'

Karen put her hand on his arm. 'No, no, don't worry. I'll be fine.'

Craig flashed his Colgate smile and looked back at the road. 'I'm dying to see her,' he said.

In the ice rink parking lot Karen immediately saw that Tawni had not come with Lawrence. Robbie's bright red pick-up truck was parked by the entrance.

Music from the rink greeted them at the door as they paid the entrance fee. While Karen rented a pair of skates, Craig put on his own and was already on the ice by the time Karen began pulling off her boots.

'Hey, look who's here!' she heard Craig sing out happily.

As scripted, Karen raised her head and looked surprised. 'Tawni, hi,' she said, forcing her voice to sound happy. 'What a coincidence.'

Tawni waved merrily. 'Robbie, you know Karen ... and Craig, from the band ...'

Karen nodded at Robbie, then lowered her head over her skates.

'Yeah, hi man,' said Robbie in his low, slow voice.

Robbie looked strikingly similar to Craig, but though he shared many of Craig's physical attributes he managed somehow to distort them, so his shiny, white-toothed smile was slightly sinister, and his straight, black hair looked slick and unwholesome.

Karen leaned her head on her knees for an instant. Robbie was not known as a talker. Perhaps tonight that was for the better. Karen felt weak and weepy for some reason. If she had to make conversation she was afraid she'd cry.

An old Beatles song came over the speakers as Karen stomped down the rubber-coated steps to the rink. Tawni flashed by her, looking cute in her red wool tights and short, short skating skirt. She'd had her kinky hair straightened and it was tied up with a red ribbon.

Gingerly, Karen slid onto the ice. Tawni wasn't all that black, she thought ruefully. She was just a shade or two darker than Craig, but Craig's father had been blunt. Craig was not to get involved with a black girl – ever.

'Come on, girl,' Craig teased Karen as he skated by, one length behind Tawni. 'Step on it. You're holding up the traffic!'

Karen waved him off and looked for Robbie. Robbie was no ace on the ice.

'Tawni's too damn fast,' Robbie said as Karen skated up to him. He was leaning against the railing. 'I'll never keep up with her. Great date, huh?'

'Craig's a lot better than me, too,' Karen recited. 'But

you and I are at about the same level.'

Robbie looked away from Tawni and ran his eyes up and down Karen's body.

'Yeah,' he grunted, and pushed off into the stream of skaters.

Karen fought for composure. I know, I know, she thought bitterly. Blue jeans and a home-knit sweater just can't match that nifty skating outfit, and neither can the body in them. But you've got no choice.

Waiting for a break in the crowd, Karen slid her way in and began skating rhythmically, keeping the speed in check. She was actually a very good skater, and sorry that the evening was going to be such a dud. At least when Tawni's sister, Jody, came no pretence was necessary. Karen enjoyed skating with her and teaching her dance steps she'd learned when she was younger. And Craig and Tawni could be together without worry.

It's so crazy, Karen thought sadly. We're all doing such dumb things for such stupid reasons. What would happen, she wondered, her anger getting the better of her and causing her to stride longer and stronger with each beat of the music, if I said: Gang, I think I'm gay. Mom, I'm in love with Allison. Or Craig said: Dad, meet my new girlfriend.

The music stopped abruptly. 'Ladies on the ice,' a man's voice boomed over the speakers. Tawni waved at Karen from the other side of the rink.

Well, Craig had already told her what would happen to

him, Karen remembered as she skated across the rink towards Tawni. First he'd get beaten up, and then grounded indefinitely. As for her, the implications were too great to conjure up.

'You okay?' Tawni asked as Karen settled into the new song alongside her. 'You look a little funny tonight.'

'I'm okay. Tired ...'

'Sorry about Robbie, he's a drag. But first I got quarantined 'cause of Jody's mumps, now she's still sick and it's been a while since Craig and I have seen each other ...'

Karen nodded. 'I know, I know, it's okay.'

'You know I appreciate it,' Tawni said softly without looking at her. 'We both do.'

'Don't say that, it's no big deal.' Karen reached over and squeezed Tawni's arm. She was hurt when Tawni pulled hastily away.

If I ever decide I'm gay it'll certainly come as no surprise to the others, Karen thought unhappily. They've already decided. Craig hadn't even thought it necessary to spell out the details of his proposal. He'd simply told her he was in love with Tawni but had to see her in secret and asked if Karen would act like his date. 'It might be worthwhile for you,' he said.

The worst thing was that Karen understood instantly what he meant, and decided on the spot that it would definitely be worth her while. She wondered fleetingly why people weren't so certain about Allison, but she knew the answer even before she finished the thought. Allison's beauty gave her the benefit of the doubt.

Now it was couples' turn. Karen paired off with a reluctant Robbie, but after just a few turns around the rink he said he was bored and walked off the ice. Karen couldn't stay without a partner, so she followed him.

'I told Tawni I hated skating,' Robbie said grumpily, sitting on a bench.

'It's not as much fun if you don't skate well,' Karen agreed without much enthusiasm.

'You don't skate so bad, little girl ...' Karen felt her cheeks flush at the insinuating sound of Robbie's voice. 'Bet you don't look all that bad either, underneath those fuddy duds.'

Karen kept her eyes on the rink, her face frozen in a nonchalant expression while her stomach turned nauseatingly.

'It true what they say?'

Robbie's face was just inches from Karen's ear, and as he leaned towards her he slid one hand onto her knee.

Karen dug her nails into her palms. Without taking her eyes off the skaters, she asked, 'What do they say?'

'That you're a lez.'

Robbie's lips were on her ear now. If she turned to look at him his mouth would touch hers.

Karen stared ahead, rigid and sick, her mind racing for an answer. 'What do you think?' she asked, her voice sounding harsher than she wanted.

'I dunno,' Robbie pulled back some. 'You look pretty shook up, but it might just be 'cause I'm the first real man you've met.' He gripped her knee, making Karen wince.

'You're hurting me,' she said, pulling away as she looked at him fearfully.

'Some girls like it.' Robbie's slow smile had a wicked bent to it.

'Well, I don't!' Karen stood up before she'd considered where to go.

'Maybe you just need to be broke in.'

Karen was so shocked by the threat, she was dumbstruck.

'Where're you going?' Craig's voice made Karen jump. 'You two tired already?'

Karen whirled around and caught Craig's searching expression. The obvious concern in his face made tears leap into Karen's eyes.

'I don't ... I feel sick,' Karen spluttered, fighting to keep from breaking into sobs.

Tawni was suddenly by her side. 'I have to go to the bathroom a sec,' Tawni said, pulling on Karen's arm. 'Come with me.'

Karen allowed herself to be led away, feeling Robbie's smirking face on her back as she went.

By the time Tawni shut the door Karen was crying quietly and convulsively into her hands.

'God, Karen, what happened? What's wrong?' Tawni hugged her, making Karen feel so grateful she was ashamed of herself.

'Robbie's a pig, Tawni. How can you stand him?' Karen said between sobs.

'He's not that bad, Karen. He just needs to be kept down with a strong hand. Lots of boys are like that. Give 'em an inch, you know – but if you don't give them the time of day they're sweet as puppies.'

'He practically threatened to rape me, Tawni.' Karen was trying to stop crying, sucking in gulps of air to calm herself.

Tawni looked at her sceptically. 'You must've misunderstood. He was probably –'

'I understood perfectly! He said I needed to be "broke in".'

Tawni looked at Karen without answering and suddenly Karen realised it wasn't that Tawni didn't believe her but that she somehow held Karen to blame. 'What did you say to him?' Tawni asked finally, as she went into one of the stalls and shut the door.

'Nothing,' Karen replied, standing alongside the row of sinks.

'Wash your face,' Tawni ordered from behind the door. 'You look awful.'

Karen turned on the faucet and splashed cold water on her face.

'You have to learn how to play the game, Karen, or you're going to get in trouble.' Tawni had come out of the stall and was now washing her hands, as Karen dried her face with a disposable towel.

Karen looked at her, feeling drained and beaten.

'All you need to do is smile, be sweet, say something nice or funny at the right moment and everything'll be all right. Don't go picking fights.'

'Why? Why smile and be sweet to jerks?' Karen objected miserably.

'Don't make waves and you won't have to deal with them.' Tawni's look seemed almost cold. 'Sure, it'd be nice not to have to. It'd be nice if Craig could take me home. But he can't. You have to be realistic.' Without saying more, Tawni walked out of the bathroom.

Karen leaned against the wall, her heart feeling as swollen and dry as her eyes. She could hear the machine smoothing out the ice for the second half of the evening, and wished she could just stand there until it was time to go. She might have attempted to except that the bathroom was filling up with noisy, chatty girls on an enforced break. Karen splashed water on her face once more, dried herself hastily, and left the bathroom.

When she got to where they had been sitting, Tawni already had her shoes on.

'Robbie's gone to turn in his skates,' Tawni said as Karen walked up. 'We're going to go.'

'It's not because of –' Karen started to say.

'I'll be sure to bring Jody next time,' interrupted Tawni.

Karen couldn't tell from the tone of her voice whether she was angry or upset, and Tawni's face gave no clues either.

Craig reached out and put his palm briefly on the side of Tawni's neck. This time, Karen caught the softness in Tawni's eyes.

'See you,' Tawni said. She turned and walked briskly to the exit.

Craig sat down heavily.

'Craig, I'm sorry,' Karen said, sitting next to him. 'It's my fault, I know, but he was scaring me and ...'

'Shhhh,' Craig sounded sad. 'It's okay. It's not you. This whole thing's stupid. I'm sorry Robbie got rough. He's a fool.'

'Tawni told you what he said?'

Craig nodded.

'Is she mad at me?' Karen wished with all her heart that she didn't care so much.

'No, she's not mad at you. She's just fed up with everything – even me, I think.'

'No, Craig. No. She loves you. I'm sure. I can see it in her eyes.'

Craig looked up.

'Just because I'm not wild about guys doesn't mean I

can't see when a girl likes somebody, Craig. It doesn't even mean I'm gay.' She was stunned that the word had come out. She'd never said anything remotely like that to anyone, except Allison.

Craig, too, seemed to realise she'd taken a road with no way back. 'You're *not* gay?' He was looking directly at her, neither pushy nor reticent, just waiting.

Let my heart flop all it wants, Karen thought, holding Craig's eyes. Craig was a friend, she was almost certain. 'I don't really know what I am,' she said from memory. 'Maybe sex just isn't for me.'

Craig nodded. 'Robbie's kind of sex isn't for me either,' he said, looking down into his lap. 'Neither is my dad's kind, up on Sunset and 9th. But Tawni ... she makes me crazy.'

Karen was stunned to see tears in his eyes. 'Oh, Craig, you're a good guy,' Karen said, hugging him impulsively.

Craig hugged her back, then seemed to pull himself together. 'What do you say we show the kids out there what two people who know how to skate look like? It's only ten-thirty.'

Karen smiled widely. 'Let's show 'em,' she said, getting to her feet. She was ready to skate the ice into water.

4

ON MONDAY MORNING KAREN WAITED FOR ALLISON by her locker, as usual, but Allison never came. She didn't show up at all that day and the first thing Karen did when she got home was to call her.

Allison's voice was hoarse over the telephone. 'Thanks for calling, Karen. I was going to wait until four to call you but you beat me to it.'

'You sound funny. Do you have a cold?'

'It feels like I'm losing my voice. I had a fever this morning but it's gone now. In fact, I feel fine but I need to write that stupid English paper for tomorrow and I really don't think I can hack it by myself. Could you come over and help me?'

'Be glad to,' Karen said. 'Just let me grab a snack and I'll be over.'

Karen was better at composition than Allison was, and she was pleased that Allison had all but admitted it. Usually it was Allison who helped Karen with her school work, so Karen was happy to return the favour. She gulped down a sandwich, grabbed her umbrella and headed off for Allison's.

The walk from the park district, where Karen lived, to the hill side of town took only fifteen minutes, but it was rainy and windy that day, slowing Karen down considerably as she struggled to hang on to her umbrella and negotiate the puddles. It was going to be a wet Christmas if the storm front held like the forecaster said it was going to. Karen couldn't remember it raining so much in Richmond and she was getting tired of grey skies. Her mother, on the other hand, never complained about the weather. Anything Tensington had to offer was better than the ten years spent in Dublin, she cheerfully reminded Karen. By the time she got to Allison's she was as wet as she would have been without an umbrella.

'Karen, you're soaked!' Allison cried out when she opened the door.

'Tell me about it,' Karen said grumpily, walking into the foyer. 'From my socks to my bra, dammit.'

Allison started giggling.

'What's so funny?'

'You look like a little orphan or something, all wet and pathetic ...'

'Fine friend you are! Would you get me something to

wear? I'm dripping all over your carpet.'

Still giggling, Allison walked down the hallway to her bedroom with Karen behind her, her feet making little squishy noises as she went. From a chest of drawers, Allison pulled out a pair of black jeans and a white sweater, thick tube socks and a pair of panties.

'I'm afraid my bras won't fit you,' Allison said, handing Karen the clothes.

'I'll do without,' Karen grumbled, tossing the clothes onto the bed. 'I hardly need one anyway.'

She pulled off her jeans, rolling them down her legs like wet cellophane, and yanked her feet out of her shoes. Stepping out of the pile of soggy panties, jeans and socks she reached over to pick up Allison's underwear. Only then did it hit her that she was half-naked in Allison's presence. Her eyes flew up to Allison's face.

Allison had a curious half-smile on her lips, and her eyes seemed more intensely blue.

Karen attributed her own involuntary shiver to a sign that she, too, was catching a cold, and rapidly pulled on Allison's clothes. When she unhooked her bra she turned her back to Allison and, heart thumping against her chest, smoothed Allison's sweater over the top of the jeans.

All better, she turned to say, but a funny lump caught in her throat and all she managed to do was squeak.

'Maybe you need hot tea,' Allison said, brushing Karen's arm as she passed. 'I wouldn't want you to catch a cold because of me.' She threw Karen a smile as she walked into the kitchen.

Karen padded down the hall behind her in Allison's socks, grateful for the break in tension. 'Where are your parents?' Karen asked, surprised at their absence at that time of day. They were usually home when she came over after school.

'They went to Bakersfield this morning,' Allison answered, putting a pot of water on the stove. 'There's a three-day workshop my mom's been planning on for months. She and Dad wanted it to be a mini-vacation. I didn't tell them I didn't feel so great this morning. They were so happy about going.'

A few minutes later they were back in Allison's room, English books and papers spread over the desk, the two of them sitting close and cosy in wicker chairs. Karen was sipping her tea, explaining to Allison how she had to put all the points she was going to address in her first paragraph, and then dedicate the subsequent paragraphs to each point before drawing her conclusion. Allison tapped her pen lightly against her notebook, trying to come to grips with what exactly she wanted to say about the poetry of Robert Frost.

'Allison, if you don't even know what you want to say how can I help you write your paper? Couldn't you have gotten some ideas from your mom? She'd be perfect, wouldn't she?'

Allison nodded. 'Of course, except that she won't say a word on the subject. She says it would end up her opinion and not mine. She's a pain when it comes to that.'

Thunder rolled across the dark sky and wind-blown raindrops splattered against the window by the desk. It was warm in Allison's room, and Karen felt calm and content, watching Allison's bent head as she attempted to write her first sentence.

Lightning lit up the horizon and a peal of thunder shook the window frame. Allison threw down her pen.

'I can't concentrate,' she said, pushing her notebook away and turning to Karen.

Instinctively, Karen knew it was not the rain or the thunder or the lightning ripping through the sky. It was her. Allison had such an intense look, her eyes seemed to be going black. Though Karen's heart skipped a beat she remained strangely calm. In fact, she looked closely at Allison's face.

'What is it, Allison?' she asked, knowing perfectly well what it was.

'You already know.' Allison's voice sounded younger, fragile in a way Karen had never heard before.

Karen's body seemed no longer under her control. Her hand reached out of its own volition and slowly and gently pushed Allison's curling red hair back off her shoulder. Though she would never have touched Allison's neck had she been in charge, that she did so did not frighten her. She thought it strange that everything about the moment felt natural. By then, her hand reached behind, underneath Allison's hair, and her body leaned forward, and they kissed. It was warm and tender, so sweet that Karen felt she wanted to indulge in it forever. Inhaling the faint smell of Allison's perfume, the clean, starched smell of her nightgown, Karen brought her hand to Allison's cheek, then slipped it down to her collar bone.

Allison stepped away. 'I've never done this before,' she whispered. She touched the ribbon at the neck of her nightgown. 'I don't know what to do.'

Karen didn't know what to do either, but she knew she wanted Allison's smooth, milky skin pressed against her own. She closed her eyes, allowing her senses to guide her, and reached out to untie the ribbon.

By the time they lay relaxed, side by side on Allison's bed, the storm had passed and it was simply raining steady and hard. The pattering sound of water on asphalt was comforting and familiar. It was dark as night but the little electric clock on Allison's night stand read six-thirty.

Feeling dreamy and distant, Karen lazily broke the long silence. 'I should call and tell Mom I'm here.' The thought of her mother brought Karen back to reality hard and fast. 'Oh, God, Allison ...' Karen sat up, pulling the sheet with her to cover her breasts. 'Oh, Allison ... what have we done?'

Allison looked at her, puzzled. Before she could say anything, Karen jumped out of bed and pulled on her clothes with furious speed, talking all the while.

'I don't believe it ... I just can't believe it. We shouldn't have ever ... never ... it isn't natural and I won't ...' She stopped long enough to pull the sweater over her head. 'You're sick, Allison,' Karen whirled on Allison, sputtering in anger. 'You planned it all from the very beginning ... I never would have ...'

'Karen, don't talk like that,' Allison started to get out of bed, tears forming in her eyes.

Karen turned her back to her. 'Cover yourself,' she said. Her voice was low and hard. It didn't sound anything like her. She bent to get her shoes.

Allison sat back down on the bed and pulled the blankets around her shoulders. 'Is that Grandma talking?' Allison asked, her voice sad.

Karen got her wet shoes on and, without a word or backward glance, gathered up her things and practically ran out of the room.

Now that she was out on the street, Karen started running up the hill towards home. Rain stung her face and she was quickly out of breath, but she forced herself to keep running, even when a sideache developed. Still she ran, as if the pain were punishment that she deserved to endure.

When she stumbled up the steps to her house she could barely breathe and it was in this condition, soaking wet and gasping for air, that her mother met her, heading out with her umbrella to check the mail.

'Darling, what happened, where've you been?' Mom dropped the umbrella on the ground and gathered her daughter into her arms.

'Oh, Mom ...' Karen tried to speak, but ended up crying out in pain.

'Are you hurt ... sweetheart, tell me, what is it?'

Karen could tell from the sound of Mom's voice that she was extremely concerned. She just had to reassure her. It took a supreme effort to let go of her mother, choke back her tears and gulp in enough air to speak.

'Okay ... I'm okay, Mom,' she managed to say. 'I got caught in the rain. Running gave me a sideache, that's all.' She managed a wan smile.

One look from her mother was enough to tell Karen that Mom knew all was not right. But Mom busied herself, helping Karen into the house, getting her into her pyjamas and making her comfortable in bed.

'I'll go make you some broth, honey,' Mom said, standing in the doorway. 'You just relax, get warm, and we'll talk after you feel better.' She seemed to want to say more, lingering there at the door, but headed off down the hallway finally, after dimming the light in Karen's room.

Though the pain soon subsided and she was quickly

warm, Karen still felt as though she couldn't talk. Beating in her brain was so much anger, worry and fear that she knew one word would bring a flood of tears and an admission of things she could never imagine saying to anyone, let alone her mother. The only escape was sleep, and she feigned it well enough to leave her mother standing there uncertainly by the bed for a few minutes, tray in hand, before sighing in resignation. She covered Karen's shoulders, kissed her sweetly on the forehead and walked out. Only then did Karen release all the pent-up emotions, crying long into the night.

5

WHEN KAREN WOKE UP IT WAS ONLY SIX O'CLOCK. Though the sky was clear and the first rays of a splendid winter sun were lighting up the horizon, Karen felt as heavy and tumultuous as the storm the day before. She didn't know how she would face her mother and was certain she couldn't go to school. It was surprising that she felt no pain in her body and was perfectly able to get out of bed and put her robe on. The way her heart felt she expected to be unable to move.

Karen walked quietly down to the kitchen and was stunned to see Mom sipping coffee at the table when she switched on the kitchen light.

'Mom ...' Karen stood in the doorway. There was nowhere to run.

'Hi, honey, how're you feeling?'

Karen nodded. 'Fine,' she said lightly, collecting herself mentally and walking casually to the table. 'Fine now.'

'I couldn't sleep,' said Mom. 'You really looked awful yesterday, like something terrible happened.'

Karen put the teapot over the flame. 'No, Mom, nothing happened except that I got caught in the rain coming home from ... Allison's.' She prayed for the strength to sound light and natural, but just saying Allison's name brought pricks of tears to her eyes.

'But you were hurting. Yes, I know, a sideache you said.' Mom spoke quickly. 'But you looked ... well, like something more than a sideache was hurting you.'

Karen consciously relaxed the muscles in her face before turning towards her mother. 'Really, Mom, I'm fine. It was dark and I was wet and my side was really killing me. I just panicked.' She smiled. 'Then, as soon as I was warm and cosy in bed, I fell asleep.' She sat down at the table, wishing there was some reason for her to be elsewhere.

Her mother looked at her searchingly. 'Well, thank goodness. You gave me a scare.' She, too, smiled, but didn't sound convinced. 'So, you're not ill or anything, no fever?'

She reached out to touch Karen's forehead but Karen jumped up as the kettle started to whistle, and said hastily, 'No, no, Mom, I'm just fine ... believe me.' The words caught in her throat as she picked up the teapot.

'Okay, okay, but let me drop you off at school this morning. It might rain again, even though it looks sunny, and I wouldn't want your side to hurt again. You know, maybe you really pulled something yesterday. It's possible, and ... oh, I'll just feel better if I drop you off, okay?'

'Sure,' Karen said, sick at heart. She'd just sealed her own fate.

In the car, Karen tried to concentrate on the scenery, on her homework, on anything but what she would do when she came face-to-face with Allison at her locker. Mom was quiet the whole drive but Karen caught her stealing glances at her every once in a while from the corner of her eye.

'Are you sure everything's okay, Karen?' Mom finally said when she pulled up in front of Seaworth High. 'I promise I won't ask you again. Just look me in the eyes and tell me you're fine.'

Karen swallowed hard, turned and looked at her mother. 'I'm fine, Mom. Really.' Then, she got out of the car and walked rapidly up the steps, listening for the sound of her mother's car driving away. She was almost at the very top of the third tier of steps when she finally heard it. There was no time, though, to savour relief, for standing at the entrance was Allison.

'Karen,' Allison called out, as she came to meet her. 'Karen, are you okay?'

Karen brushed past her and walked into the building. Allison was at her right shoulder as Karen neared her locker.

'Karen, please, we need to talk.'

Resolutely, Karen turned to look at her. There were

dark circles under Allison's eyes, and her hair was pulled into a tight, unnatural knot at the nape of her neck. Allison's tremulous smile cut into Karen's heart, but Karen forced herself to say what she knew she must.

'We're not going to talk and we're not going to see each other again. I'll ask Administration to give me another locker, closer to my classes or something, and I'll drop drama workshop until next quarter. The rest of the time ...' She couldn't go on. The hurt in Allison's eyes was breaking her heart.

'We can't be friends?' Allison was practically whispering.

Karen busied herself with something in her locker.

'Please, Karen, don't listen to what others say. Listen to what *you* say, inside. We didn't do anything –'

Karen slammed her locker closed and walked briskly away.

'– wrong.'

It was the longest day in Karen's life. When she wasn't willing herself to keep her eyes off Allison during the classes they shared, she was trying not to see her face during the classes they didn't share. She hid out in the study hall during lunch and excused herself early from French, saying she was ill, so that she could leave school a good fifteen minutes early. She felt so utterly tormented by the time she got home that she lost control and cried long and loudly until she felt drained. For the first time, ever, she wanted to get drunk, to numb all the thoughts going on in her mind.

Was she gay? A lesbian? Nobody in her house had ever said so, but Karen was sure that being a lesbian was like being a criminal. Worse! Grandma wouldn't allow it. And her father? God, Dad would kill her.

Karen smiled in spite of herself. Grandma was dead, she reminded herself. Dead for good. And Dad probably couldn't even remember how old she was.

The phone rang and Karen stiffened. It's her, she thought. Don't answer.

It rang and rang, stopped, then began ringing again.

It could have been Mom, Karen thought guiltily, worried as she had been that morning. Karen ran over to the kitchen phone and picked it up. 'Yes?'

'Oh, good, you're home.' It was Mom. 'I was starting to worry.'

Karen said nothing, and her mother filled the silence.

'I just wanted to be sure you're home and all right, that's all. I'll be home a little earlier this evening, okay?' She paused. 'Dad's in town. Just passing through on his way to a new assignment. Some bridge repair. He wanted us all to have dinner together. I'll just get some take-away.' Her mother's voice faded, obviously not any more thrilled about this prospect than Karen.

'Oh,' Karen said, more quietly than she meant to. 'Yes, okay,' she said, stronger. 'See you later.' She hung up without waiting for her mother to say goodbye. This she did not need, Karen thought unhappily, trudging to her room to change. Now, instead of making as short an evening as possible of the time left in the day she was going to have to go through her father's third degree. Since he saw them so rarely he grilled them about school, grades, friends and hobbies as though they had to pass some sort of entrance exam. At the best of times it was gruelling, now it was going to be horrendous.

Karen was still in her room, pulling on a decent sweatsuit her father would have no cause to criticise, when she heard Danny's voice booming from the front walk.

'You really said that, Dad?' she heard him say at the same time as the key turned in the front-door lock.

'I certainly did.' It was her father's voice. 'Told him to buzz off.'

They were walking in the doorway. Karen's heart dropped. Facing her father right now was going to be extraordinarily difficult, but without her mother there to take the brunt of his attention off her it was going to be death-defying. Feeling like an animal facing slaughter, Karen gave a half-hearted glance at herself in the mirror. She couldn't hide in her room. Might as well face the music.

'Well, little lady,' Dad practically shouted when Karen appeared in the living room, 'you're getting tall.' He went to hug her. His pleasure was so genuine Karen felt a tiny bit better, but the feeling was short-lived. 'So? Who's the lucky fella?' He had stepped away from her but was still holding her by the shoulders and looking into her face expectantly. The smile that played on his mouth seemed less than innocent.

'Oh! Nobody that special,' Karen hazarded, trying to break his gaze by nodding at the couch. 'Sit and relax. Mom'll be here any minute, I'm sure.'

But her father did not relent. 'I've been sitting on a plane for five hours,' he said jovially. 'My backside's numb!'

Danny guffawed and his father rewarded him with a thump on the back.

Karen felt her shoulders slumping along with her plummeting upper lip. This was going to be even harder than she had expected.

'So, nobody special?' he persisted.

'She sees more of her friend Allison than any boyfriend,' Danny teased from the armchair. 'Karen's a late bloomer!'

Danny laughed but Dad looked at Karen closely. 'You're getting on, Karen, not a child anymore. In my day girls were getting married at your age.'

'It's not like that here, Dad,' Karen said, trying to keep her voice even. 'In America.'

'Now don't try to tell me America's that different from Ireland,' her father interrupted. He let go of her shoulders and sat down on the couch. 'Times have changed everywhere. I just thought you'd have someone special by now. Danny's seeing a girl ...'

Karen glanced over at her brother. She had never once heard him mention a girlfriend.

Danny looked sheepish and continued needling Karen. 'She probably knows the inside of Allison's house better than ours.'

'Oh shut up!' Karen burst out, feeling hemmed in and angry. 'That's not true. In fact, we aren't friends anymore. We had a fight.' She had blurted out more than she had time to think through and only the sceptical look on her brother's face kept her talking. 'Allison says I took Craig away from her and that if I'm not willing to give him up she doesn't want to be my friend!'

Now her brother looked positively astounded and Karen, feeling guilty and frightened by the immensity of her lie, continued recklessly, unable now to stop. 'I've been seeing a guy named Craig Ferrante.' She looked at her father. 'He's in a band. He plays the tuba. And Allison said she liked him first but really it was me and so ...'

Her father's puzzled expression stopped her. She knew she sounded like a third-grader, and she felt herself blushing so fiercely she had broken out in a sweat. Why on earth hadn't she just kept quiet?

The sound of the front door opening was music to Karen's ears. 'It's Mom,' she said, unnecessarily. 'Mom, let me help you.' And she ran to the door to take the bag out of her mother's arms without even giving her a chance to put her purse down.

'Goodness,' Mom exclaimed as Karen disappeared rapidly into the kitchen. Danny and Dad had come into the hall. 'Patrick,' Mom said, nodding in Dad's direction. 'You're looking well.'

'Fit as a fiddle. And you, Carol? Have a hard day at the office, dear?' He said it with a smirk.

'You'd think I leave an hour early on a daily basis – the fuss they made!' Mom refused to take the bait. She put down her purse and hung up her coat. 'I stopped and got some Chinese take-away. Karen is probably setting the table.' Without waiting for a response she headed for the kitchen.

Dad winked at Danny and they followed her.

'How are you?' Mom said softly over Karen's shoulder before the others walked into the kitchen. 'I've been thinking about you all day.'

'Fine, Mom, really. You got so much stuff!' Karen was setting out the white cardboard containers on the table, opening each one and putting in a serving spoon the way they always did when they ate Chinese.

'All a bit dramatic here, isn't it?' Dad said heartily, as soon as they had said Grace and begun to spoon steamed rice onto their plates. Karen stared down into her plate as her mother looked at him questioningly.

'Karen had a fight with her friend – Allison, was it? Over a boy.'

Mom looked quickly over at Karen. 'Is that true?'

Karen nodded.

'Karen's standing by her man so Allison broke off their friendship.' Danny was enjoying Karen's discomfort immensely.

'Allison did that?' Obviously, Mom was finding this hard to believe. 'Over Craig?'

'That was the name. Craig Ferrante. Mexican, is he?'

'Half-and-half,' Danny answered for Karen. 'Half-Irish.' He knew his father would approve.

'Is that so? You did the right thing,' Dad assured Karen.

Karen felt like breaking into tears but had the presence of mind to point to her full mouth as an excuse for not speaking.

'That doesn't sound at all like Allison,' Mom mused.

'Girls always pull out the claws when it comes to boys,' Dad said. 'It's natural.'

'So, what's the new job, Patrick?' Mom asked, fearing the direction this conversation was leading.

'The Golden Gate!' Danny said happily, as if he were going there himself.

Their father glowed from the obvious pride in Danny's demeanour and leaned back to recount the frantic phone calls and phenomenal wages – all in order to have him, the best trainer in the field of underwater construction, come to the pride of the Golden State and teach a new crop of maintenance workers the secrets of his trade. It wasn't the most interesting discussion but it did take his attention away from Karen and she capitalised as best she could by asking as many questions as possible.

She could sense her mother look at her now and then, uncomfortable with Karen's behaviour, but she ignored her and commiserated with her father about the long hours and dangerous conditions of his job. By the time the conversation wound down, a full hour and a half had gone by and their father was pushing back his chair to stand.

'Sorry to eat and run,' he said, wiping his mouth with a napkin. 'I would have liked to talk more about what you two are doing, but I got carried away instead. Still, I have a flight to catch.'

'That's okay, Dad,' Danny stood up too. 'I'll call you a cab.'

'Now that we're going to be so close for the next couple of months I'll be able to come over more often,' Dad said, putting on his jacket. 'We have a lot of lost time to catch up on.'

'Okay, Dad.' Karen was feeling weak and hollow.

'Are you sure this girl's all right?' Dad said to Mom. 'She looks a bit pale to me.'

'Perhaps just tired,' Mom said lightly, but the concern in her eyes was a giveaway.

'Has she been sick? Is she eating properly? Not on any

of those crazy diets, is she?'

'No, no,' Karen said, to take the pressure off her mother. 'I'm just tired. This is my senior year, you know. It's pretty tough.'

'Get enough rest,' her father said as they walked him to the door. 'Eat properly, get enough rest and – don't worry about Allison. It's just a part of life.' He hugged Karen at the door, then said to Mom: 'I'll call you, Carol. Perhaps the kids can come up for a weekend? San Francisco's a great city.'

Mom nodded.

'I'll wait outside with you for the cab,' Danny interjected before she could say anything. He seemed anxious for some time alone with his father.

'Right, so,' said Dad. 'Talk to you all soon.' And the two of them walked out into the porch and shut the door behind them.

Karen turned to go to her room, but her mother stopped her. 'Honey, what's this about Allison? I can't get over what your father said. It just doesn't seem like her.'

'Oh, she's changed a lot, Mom. She's been getting harder to get along with ... but we can talk later. I really am tired.'

'Is that what's been eating at you then? What upset you yesterday?' Mom had put her hand on Karen's shoulder and though she was not holding her back Karen knew she could not leave.

'That's what it was.' Hoping that her face was a blank mask, she looked directly into her mother's face. Every inch of her body wanted to turn away and race into her bedroom but she held Mom's eyes until her mother looked away.

'I hope she'll get over such a silly notion.' Mom had released her shoulder and though it was clear that Karen could leave the room now, her mother continued talking, almost to herself. 'Perhaps we could invite her family over, get to know each other better ... maybe it would help to –'

'Let things run their course, Mom,' Karen interrupted. 'I'm sure she'll get over it eventually.' She smiled convincingly and rubbed her face. 'I'm so exhausted. See you in the morning, okay?'

When her mother didn't answer Karen stepped closer and kissed her on the cheek. Mom absentmindedly kissed her back. ''Night, Karen.'

Karen walked down the hall, leaving her mother standing in the middle of the living room, as if still thinking about what Karen had said. Karen stopped at her bedroom door, half-tempted to go back and try to banish all doubt from her mother's mind, but she couldn't face another minute of this never-ending day. 'I want everything back to normal,' Karen said softly to her reflection in the bedroom mirror. 'School, friends – and boys,' she forced herself to say. 'Boys,' she made herself say again.

Neither brushing her teeth nor washing her face, Karen simply threw off her clothes and crawled into bed, body stone-tired but mind wired and buzzing. What she wanted more than anything was to drop instantly into a deep sleep, the way babies do before you've even pulled the blankets to their chins, but nothing of the sort happened, and she lay wide awake, hearing Danny walk back into the house and get ready noisily for bed. Then it was her mother's turn, but instead of going to bed she sat in the kitchen and called somebody named Albert on the phone.

Karen wasn't nosy and would normally not have attempted to listen in on her mother's side of a conversation. Now she couldn't help it, and though Mom was keeping her voice down, it carried through the still, quiet house.

She had never mentioned anybody called Albert, Karen thought to herself, noticing the gentleness in her mother's voice. Maybe she's in love and doesn't know how to tell Grandma!

'No, no, Albert, everything's just fine. Patrick was here and dinner went smoothly,' Karen heard her mother lie. 'And Karen seems fine now – something about a boy. Nothing serious. You know, first love ...'

Fleetingly Karen wondered why her mother was playing down the gloom of the evening, but as she heard their conversation veer into work and deadlines, she finally drifted off to sleep. 'That's what I have to do,' she murmured as she snuggled down under the blankets. 'Find a boy and fall in love. It can't be that hard.'

6

FINDING A BOY PROVED A LOT HARDER than Karen thought it would be. She knew exactly what to do but it was her body, her voice, her choice of words that seemed to sabotage her at every occasion. She'd mean to smile sweetly at the captain of the football team and start to cry instead. She learned a joke to amuse Roger during study and forget the punch-line half-way through. Her hand shook if she reached out to touch someone on the shoulder and she stumbled when she tried to walk sexily to the drinking fountain during lunch one day. It got so she was terrified of any kind of personal contact and she started to avoid people almost as much as they began avoiding her.

There was no respite at home, either. She couldn't seem to concentrate on her school work. She re-read entire chapters again and again, frightened by the realisation that nothing whatsoever was sinking in. What seemed like a few minutes of day-dreaming at her desk ended up being hours, and she began to get warning notes from her teachers which she didn't show to her mother.

Making matters worse was that her father was true to his word. They were in the same state now and he began to call them every evening, instead of once a month, and to send airfare for weekend trips to San Francisco. Danny was taking advantage of every minute and his efforts at adopting a manly persona intensified. Karen could beg off with the excuse of upcoming mid-term exams but she knew that come the Christmas holidays nothing could save her from spending time with her father. She felt guilty about avoiding his calls and making up excuses, but her mind was in a turmoil and she was acting now out of self-preservation.

The intense effort to act at least half-way normal at school and totally upbeat at home took its toll. Karen began to suffer from piercing migraine headaches and bouts of insatiable hunger. Though she laughed away her eating binges by using them as proof to her mother that she was, in fact, as healthy and happy as a horse, deep inside Karen knew she was losing control.

The Saturday before mid-term exams, Karen lay in bed, unable to get up and face the day. She knew she had to collect herself, study hard and block out the chaos reigning in her mind. She had to become, once more, a diligent student and a good girl. If only she could quiet the endless rattling in her head.

A lez ... a lez ... She realised the word was invading her thoughts. Gay. Criminally gay, grossly depraved ... a dyke. Oh, God, stop it! Karen almost shouted, jumping out of bed.

'I'm going to have breakfast, now,' Karen mumbled to herself, throwing on her robe. 'I'll have one egg and one slice of toast, one glass of orange juice, then I'll dress and hit the books,' she told herself as she walked out of her room, 'Geography first, then history, then English and French,' but it didn't drown out the little voice in her head singing cruelly: Is it true what they say ... is it true that you're gay?

'Hi! I was wondering when you were going to get up.' Mom was making coffee in the kitchen, already dressed. 'You know I'm taking Danny to the airport – are you sure you don't want to go this time either?'

'What? No, I ... yes, I need to study.' Karen went straight to the refrigerator and got an egg.

'Give yourself a rest, sweetheart. You've been bent over your books every afternoon for the last couple of weeks. Surely you don't have to spend every waking moment studying. What's there is there and what isn't won't be. You could use a break, and a trip to San Francisco might be lots of fun.'

'I have to study a lot, Mom. I want to do well in my first tests in this school. Damn! I got eggshell in my bowl.'

'Here, I can get it –'

'No, forget it, I'll just add another egg.'

'I don't think that's going –'

'Sure it'll help. The omelette will be thicker.'

Karen grabbed another egg, broke it into the bowl and began beating the eggs with a fork. 'English and French, English and French,' she muttered, as she turned to the stove. 'French toast, French kiss ...'

'What are you mumbling, Karen?'

'Nothing, nothing! My classes ... what I'm going to do first.'

'Do you want some toast? I'm making myself some.'

'Yes, one slice ... no, two. Two, okay?'

'Yes, okay, two slices for you ...' Mom put the bread into the toaster, looking perplexed. 'You know, I don't usually push you about seeing your father but you seem to be avoiding him. Are you sure everything's okay?'

'Of course, Mom. Don't you want me to get good grades?'

Her mother sighed. 'Know what I was thinking, Karen?'

Karen turned slightly from the stove as she poured the eggs into a small skillet.

'I'm thinking of asking for a few days off, right before Christmas, so we can do something really festive this year, like have a tree-decorating party, invite all your friends, make egg-nog, you know ...'

'Oh, Mom, I don't think that's such a great idea. Lots of

people are leaving for the holidays, and who goes to a tree-decorating party anyway? It's childish, Mom.'

'You really think that? I can't imagine people feeling that way. It's part of the Christmas spirit and a good way to get friends together. I was thinking we could invite Allison and –'

'No!' Karen whirled away from the stove and practically threw herself onto the table. 'No,' she said more calmly, trying to get a hold of herself. 'I'm not a baby, Mom. I don't need you to patch up my fights for me.'

'I know, I just thought ...'

'I'm not interested, Mom, not if that's why you want to do it.'

'That's not the only reason.' Mom began pacing the kitchen. 'We don't have to invite her, though I still think it's a shame you don't want to try to make up. I also wanted to have the party because ... because I'd like to have you meet some of my friends, a special friend in particular.'

Karen turned back to the stove and flipped over the omelette. 'Sure, Mom, I'd like to meet your friends. Is the toast ready?'

Mom stared at her for an instant before popping up the toaster. 'Yes, here,' she said, handing Karen two slices. 'You'll help me, then?'

'With what?' Karen brought her breakfast to the table.

'Plan the party, get what we need, cook.'

'Yeah, sure. Do we have any chocolate milk?'

Her mother nodded.

'You just write me a list of the things you need and I'll buy them,' Karen continued, as she fiddled with the milk and NesQuick.

'Actually, I thought we could shop together, and cook, you know, have fun planning. Heavens, Karen, are you going to put all that chocolate in there? You didn't use to have such big breakfasts.'

'Guess I'm still a growing girl. Okay, you tell me when you want to shop or whatever.' Karen dug into her breakfast.

'Come on, Mom. We'll be late.' Danny had rushed into the kitchen, still buckling his belt.

'Just finishing my coffee,' Mom said. 'Don't you want a piece of toast or something?'

'No. They give us something on the plane and then Dad said he'd take me to a truck stop for brunch.'

'A truck stop? Big spender,' muttered Karen.

'What did Dad ever do to you?' Danny turned on his sister. 'It's food just like what you're stuffing your face with and it's close to Dad's site. You've been really mean, lately, and weirder than anything.'

Karen dropped her head. She knew her brother was right but she couldn't admit it. 'You're just a freshman. What do you know about senior exams?'

'Let's go, Danny,' Mom interjected. 'Karen has been quite tense but once these tests are over things will calm down. Won't they, Karen?'

Karen nodded without raising her head. Her mother sighed and turned to the doorway. 'I won't be long. About half an hour.'

'Sure,' Karen said, her mouth full of food.

Hesitating an instant by the door, Mom looked at Karen, then walked out of the kitchen. Danny glared at her before following but he didn't say more. In a few seconds the door closed behind them.

Karen ploughed through her breakfast, put the dishes into the sink, grabbed some cookies out of the cookie jar and went back to her room. She dressed, munching on Oreos, put her school books on her desk and sat down to study. Methodically, she ate her way through the bag of cookies as she read the assigned chapters in her geography book. The postman rang the bell, and someone telephoned, but all Karen really heard were the words of her subconscious.

You're gay.

I'm not!

You love Allison.

I don't!

You just need to be broke in.

Karen looked up. The empty cookie bag lay crumpled by her book, still open at page one. She'd accidentally spilled some milk on her desk and the puddle reached the edges of her French notebook.

'Oh, damn!' Karen said aloud, shoving her books and

notebooks to one side. 'Damn!' Tears filled her eyes. She pushed away from the desk and walked briskly to her closet. Pulling out her jacket, she struggled into it as she walked down the hall and out of the house, leaving her purse and keys and, she prayed, her thoughts behind the closed door.

Walking hurriedly down the block, Karen went where her feet took her, bending her head against the biting wind. Shop windows were bedecked in Christmas colours and carols could be heard coming from everywhere. Shoppers crowded the sidewalks, Santa Clauses rang bells and gaily decorated trees lined the avenues. Karen passed all this without seeing it, until she raised her head and noticed that she had no idea where she was. She'd left the shopping district a good way back and was now walking through a posh-looking neighbourhood, with stately homes which seemed to have been sub-divided into small but chic apartments, with lots of manicured lawns and flower-beds.

Karen stopped and looked around. She had no idea how much time had passed since she left her house and was certain she'd never seen this part of town before. Walking more slowly, Karen headed for the corner in order to read the street sign.

Thirty-second and Kincaid. There was no doubt now that she'd never gone this far east. Holding her collar close against her neck, Karen turned to walk back the way she had come when she heard someone calling.

'Hey! Hey, you!'

Karen decided nobody could be speaking to her here so she kept on walking. Then she heard it again.

'Hey, Karen!'

Karen stopped and turned. This time she could see somebody walking towards her from a parked car. Robbie.

'Watcha doin' here, girl?' Robbie wore a black leather jacket, tight black pants and a cap perched on the side of his head. Karen knew that every single piece of his outfit cost a fortune.

'Hi,' said Karen, trying to smile in a friendly fashion. 'Believe it or not I got lost. I was just trying to make my way back home.'

'Where do you live?' Robbie kept coming closer, forcing Karen to back up until she was standing against a brick building. He stopped right in front of her and leaned one hand on the wall by her head.

'The Park district,' Karen replied, pressing against the wall as she began to feel uncomfortable.

'And you're way out here?' Robbie's smile looked malicious.

'Yeah, well, I'd better head on home.' Karen attempted to side-step Robbie but he took hold of her arm.

'Hold on, now. It'll take you an hour on foot. Me and my brother can give you a lift, right to your own front door. How's that for service?' He paused as Karen looked up and down the deserted street. 'Or does hangin' out with two cool dudes gross you out?'

'Not in the least,' said Karen, her cheeks beginning to burn. 'Wouldn't want you to have to go out of your way, that's all.'

'No trouble too great for a nice little girl like you,' said Robbie, pulling her away from the building. 'You'll like going in style.' He nodded to a sleek, black Porsche parked across the street.

What else can I do, Karen thought, angry at the alarm bells going off in her head. There's not a soul around. If he wanted to he could just drag me into the car. At least this way I have room to manoeuvre. 'Real nice,' she said, when Robbie opened the door to the back seat. The car had leather seats and huge speakers.

'Knew you'd like it.' Robbie closed the door and got into the passenger side. 'This is Richie.' He patted his brother's shoulder.

'Nice to meet you,' Karen said, ever so politely.

Richie tipped his cap to her without saying anything.

'This nice thing lives in the Park district,' Robbie said, as Richie started the engine. 'We're going to give her a lift home.' Without commenting, Richie pulled away from the curb. 'Some music?' Without waiting for her to answer, Robbie selected a tape and slid it into the tape deck. Heavy Metal filled the car, rattling the windows.

Though Richie drove along Thirty-second Street, Karen noticed that he began to make more turns than she thought necessary.

'Are you sure we're going to the Park district?' she said loudly, leaning forward.

Nobody answered.

Karen timidly tapped Robbie on the shoulder. 'Are you sure this is the way?'

'Sure, yeah,' Robbie nodded.

Karen had lost all sense of direction. I can always just get out when he stops, she thought, looking for a place with more people. Karen put her hand on the door handle, waiting for the right moment, when suddenly the car swerved to the right and came to a halt by the curb. In that same instant, Robbie turned the music off.

Karen saw immediately that this street was as deserted as the others. 'Where are we?' she asked, trying to sound nonchalant.

'My house,' said Robbie, getting out. He came over and opened the back door.

'Weren't we going to ... my house?' Karen didn't move.

'Richie's got to run an errand first, and some friends are over I want you to meet. When he's done we'll take you home.'

Richie's revving the engine impatiently got Karen out of the car. Robbie had barely shut the door before Richie screeched off down the street.

'This way, please,' said Robbie, bowing in mock subservience.

Karen hesitated.

'We're having a party.' Robbie straightened. 'If I don't turn you on you'll meet somebody that do.'

Karen willed herself to smile. This is your chance, she thought grimly, walking into the elegant foyer of the building. Prove yourself.

Though Karen had no idea where she was, Robbie insisted she precede him up the stairs, nudging her along from behind to keep her climbing until they'd reached the second floor.

'To the right,' he directed her, then took her arm and stopped her in front of apartment 37.

It was dark in the hall, the walls lined in velvet wallpaper, and equally dark in the apartment as Robbie opened the door.

Play the game, Karen ordered herself, as Robbie nudged her in. Learn to play the game.

Trying to see the dim interior, Karen took in her surroundings. Curtains were drawn over two sets of windows, with only a bit of light coming through the slits in the fabric. There were some people sitting on an elegant, low, white couch and others on the floor, strewn about the white shag carpet or leaning against the walls. Music was playing quietly somewhere and the air was filled with smoke.

'This is my friend Karen,' Robbie announced, as he closed the door behind her.

Some of them glanced up but nobody said anything.

A girl walked in from another part of the apartment. Karen recognised Lea, from the cheerleading squad.

'Hey, Lea, you know Karen,' said Robbie.

'Hi,' said Karen, glad to see a familiar face.

Lea nodded. 'Did you bring the stuff?' she asked Robbie.

'Richie's gone now to get it. Five minutes, tops.'

Lea turned as a boy came from the hall. 'Five minutes, Chuckie,' she said.

Chuck took Lea by the shoulders and kissed her neck. 'I can wait,' he said, sliding his hands beneath her sweater. 'Can you?'

Lea giggled. 'You just hang on, now,' she said, her voice husky, pulling his hands down. 'Five minutes won't kill you.'

Chuck laughed, turned her to face him and kissed her mouth.

Karen looked away and found Robbie staring at her with a funny expression on his face.

'Nice and warm in here,' Karen said, trying to make conversation in order to calm her pounding heart.

'Take your jacket off, then,' said Robbie, smiling that wicked smile of his.

'Oh, I, well ... maybe I'll just keep it on for ...' Robbie reached out and had her jacket unzipped and half-off before she could finish. 'I'll put it right here,' he said, laying it across a white wicker chair. 'Go on in.' He nudged her towards the hall.

Karen was relieved to find herself in the kitchen.

'Want a drink?' Robbie opened the fridge. It was full of beers and fancy, gourmet food.

Karen began to shake her head no, but changed her mind. 'Thanks,' she said. Anything to buy time. Robbie snapped a can of beer off from the plastic liner. She opened the tab and took a long drink. The bitter taste made her shudder but she took another long swig, this time looking at Robbie.

'You live really far from school,' she said.

He nodded.

'Does it take you long to drive?' She knew she sounded inane but she could think of nothing else to say.

'Not too bad,' Robbie said.

Karen took another sip, then set the can on the counter. She hated beer.

'No more?'

'Uh, no, thanks. Never did like beer much ...'

'Maybe you'll like what Richie's bringing.' Robbie was looking her up and down, biting his lower lip.

'I didn't come here for drugs,' said Karen, trying to sound cool.

'No?' Robbie came closer.

It took superhuman strength not to run as Robbie reached out and put his hand on Karen's hip.

'No?' He smiled, then pulled her close, roughly, and kissed her mouth.

Let him, Karen thought. Relax, you'll like it, she commanded herself. Then his tongue pushed through her lips and Karen pulled away.

'Whoa ...' she said, backing into the kitchen door. 'Let's not rush.' She hoped she'd said it sweetly. 'Why don't you show me the rest of the apartment? It's really beautiful.' And she opened the kitchen door and slipped out, Robbie right behind her.

'I make you nervous, don't I,' Robbie said, as she walked back into the living room.

'A girl needs some time,' Karen said coyly.

'Time ... or another girl, maybe,' said Robbie into her ear.

Karen forced herself to lean her back against Robbie's body. 'Time,' she said.

'You've got three minutes and twenty-one seconds,' Robbie said. 'Then Richie'll be here and I'll be a changed dude.'

Karen made her way through the living room with Robbie hot on her heels, stepping over bodies that didn't move. She knew time was running out.

Now or never, she thought, walking into the hall leading to the bedrooms. 'Is this your room?' she asked out loud, stopping before a partially opened door.

'Mom's.' Robbie was now holding her shoulder, pushing slightly to keep her going down the hall.

'Looks big.' Karen stuck her head in the door, trying

anything to hold on to the minutes she had left. Suddenly she realised that there were people in the bed, three or four people, talking and giggling in hushed tones.

'Oh, my, I'm sorry.' Karen pulled her head out and quickly shut the door.

'Surprise, surprise!' said Robbie.

Karen felt the warning jabs of a migraine headache. Robbie had pushed her over to the next door and nudged her inside.

Be brave, dammit, Karen thought, fighting for self-control. All girls do it. Just make it right. 'I think it'll be nicer in the dark,' Karen said sexily in a last-ditch effort to stay on top of the situation. Now, her headache was really hurting.

'If you say so, little girl.' Robbie shut the door and put his big hands on either side of her head. He began kissing her mouth, lifting her face to receive him.

Karen put her hands on his chest and tried to push him away gently, but he tightened his grip on her head and nailed her back to the closet door with his hip. If shouts hadn't erupted from the living room at that instant, Karen felt she would have suffocated.

Robbie let go of her and walked to the door, listening. 'It's Richie with the stash.'

Her head aflame, Karen hugged her body and pressed up against the closet as if she could somehow pass through it like a ghost. 'Are you going to go get some?' she asked. Her voice seemed to be coming from elsewhere.

'Later,' Robbie shook his head. Mistaking Karen's sudden intake of breath for arousal, Robbie gave her a cocky smile and began unbuckling his belt. 'We gonna have fun now,' he said in a low, cruel-sounding voice, as he slowly pulled his belt through the belt loops. 'Robbie's kind of fun.'

Sheer terror coursed through Karen's body and, without knowing what she was doing, she sprang away from the closet screaming bloody murder. She flew through the room, out the door and hurtled down the hall, shrieking like a mad woman.

'Stop her!' Robbie shouted, as Karen streaked through the living room to the front door.

It all happened too fast for anyone in the living room to react. Karen reached the front door, threw it open and ran into the hall. Though she was totally disoriented and couldn't remember which way the stairs were, there was no time for her to think about it. She raced down the hallway, praying she was going in the right direction.

'Stop, you bitch!' she heard Robbie shouting behind her. 'You can't get away!'

Karen resisted the urge to look over her shoulder and ran on blindly, tears streaming down her face. She turned the corner and pulled up short. It was a dead end. Looking wildly right and left she saw a door with 'Stairs' written on it. She flung it open just as Robbie turned the corner.

'You can't get away, you know,' she heard him shout as

she ran up the narrow steps. She knew she was heading for the roof but there was no place else to go.

Another door, and Karen found herself on the roof-top, surrounded by large wooden flower boxes, deck chairs and potted palms. To the left was an overhang formed by another part of the building. It looked like a storage area, cluttered with gardening tools and more deck chairs. Breathless, Karen ran over and slid behind a pile of chairs, snagging her skin on protruding nails.

From where she crouched, Karen could see Robbie burst through the roof door. He took a few steps, and stopped.

'Ain't nobody else up here, girl,' he said. 'Nobody gonna save you. Nobody gonna hear you. Jus' me, and I'm mad angry.' He took a few more steps and stopped again.

Karen held her breath. She was shaking uncontrollably. The wind was icy on her skin.

'Not too many places you can hide, girl.' Robbie wasn't moving. 'I'll give you a choice, 'cause it's damn cold up here. Either you come on out and make me happy – or I'm gonna come lookin' for you. And when I find you ... I'm gonna throw you off the roof. You hear me? What Robbie wants, Robbie gets!'

God help me, God help me, raced Karen's mind. What do I do?

'You got three seconds to decide, girl!'

My God, I'm going to die here, thought Karen. Her legs

were numb and her body ached from the cold. I can't move, I can't run, there's nowhere to hide.

'Time's up!' Robbie suddenly walked briskly to the far side of the roof and leaned over the edge. 'Not on the fire escape,' he said, heading now for a pile of boxes not far from the fire escape. 'Not here,' he announced, kicking the pile apart. 'You hiding in the plants, little girl?' Karen could hear him say as he left her line of vision.

Now! Now, Karen urged her unresponding body.

'Maybe I'll just string you up from the solar panels.' Robbie's voice seemed to be on the far side of the roof.

With all the strength she could muster Karen rolled through the pile of deck chairs, scattering them in all directions, staggered to her feet and stumbled over to where she thought the fire escape was.

'I got you now!' Robbie yelled, but Karen didn't see him. She ran to the edge of the roof, sat down on the side and slid off, just as Robbie reached out and missed grabbing her hair by inches.

Landing on the platform, Karen scrambled on her hands and knees to the iron ladder, slipping and sliding down the rungs as Robbie jumped to the platform after her.

'God damn you, girl,' Robbie spluttered in rage, climbing down the fire escape. 'I'm gonna get you! Teach you not to mess with me! I'm gonna drag you into that house and let everybody in there have a go at you! Every damn one!'

With numb fingers and aching legs, Karen climbed furiously down the fire escape, jumping the last rungs to the platform. He's faster, he's faster, she thought desperately as Robbie just missed her, pulling out a fistful of her hair. Letting go half-way down, Karen crashed to the sidewalk. Pain shot up her left leg but somehow she heaved herself to her feet and ran into the street.

The sound of screeching brakes brought her to a standstill just as Robbie jumped to the ground. Karen suddenly realised she knew the person staring at her from behind the wheel.

'Get over here, girl!' she heard Robbie yell from behind her.

She ran around to the passenger side of the car, opened the door and threw herself in. 'Go, go!' she screamed at Craig. 'Drive!'

Craig looked over at Robbie running towards the car, then quickly threw the engine into gear and jerked forward. Hitting the gas he sped off, leaving Robbie yelling behind him in the middle of the street.

Karen sobbed uncontrollably, curled up in a ball on the seat next to Craig. He drove rapidly without a word, going through the intersections as fast as he could. When he finally stopped, Karen saw that they were in front of a police station.

Craig turned off the engine, took his jacket off and put it around Karen's shoulders. 'What happened, Karen?'

'Oh Craig, Oh God ...' Karen couldn't speak she was shaking and crying so hard.

Craig put his arm around her shoulders. 'Okay, just get it all out. Are you hurt?'

Karen shook her head.

'Should we go in there?' He nodded towards the police station.

Karen shook her head again.

It seemed to take hours to cry herself out, but Craig sat with his arm around her until she began to calm down.

'I was so stupid, Craig. I did such a stupid thing.'

'You went someplace with Robbie?'

'I know it sounds crazy but I didn't really have much choice – partly. And partly ... partly, I wanted to prove that ...' She started to cry.

'That you're not gay?'

Karen nodded.

'Oh, Karen,' Craig sighed.

'I got lost in his neighbourhood and he said he'd drive me home. There wasn't anybody on the street, nobody could help me if I didn't just go ...'

'So you went with him.'

'He took me to his house and said we had to go in. There was never anybody I could ask for help and I thought maybe ... if I was brave and learned how to play the game ...'

'Did Tawni tell you that – about playing the game?'

'Maybe. Why?'

'It's just something she says.'

'I was wrong. I can't play the game! So I ran and hid and he tried to catch me. He said he'd throw me off the roof or have all the people in his house rape me and ...'

'But you got away.'

'I wouldn't have, if you hadn't been there. He would have ...' Karen dropped her head and the tears started again, quiet and bitter now.

'You don't have to prove anything to anybody, Karen. Who cares what people think? You know you're not gay ...'

'But I am!' Karen jerked her head up, flushed with sudden anger. 'I'm a dyke, Craig! Are you still my friend?'

At the sight of Craig's puzzled expression, Karen dropped her head again. 'I had sex with Allison.' Her voice was barely above a whisper. 'We had ...'

'You made love.'

Karen looked at him.

'When you like somebody it's called making love.'

'You're not grossed out?'

Craig chuckled. 'No. I can't say why, considering the way I've been raised. But it doesn't bother me. Maybe because I've been trying to think with my own head lately.'

'What do you mean?'

'It's hard to explain. I just look at things and say, Craig, how do *you* feel about that?'

It was Karen's turn to look puzzled.

'It's my birthday today,' said Craig, as if that

explained everything. 'The big eighteen. I flunked a year, in case you're wondering.' She hadn't been. 'But we're not having a party. No cake, no presents. I left home. That's why I'm driving around town in my uncle's car. I'm looking for a place that doesn't want six months' rent in advance, but I drove over here just to daydream. I'd like to make it out here, some day.'

'You mean you left home for good?'

Craig nodded. 'I can't live the way Dad wants. I can't look at things with his head. It's been making me sick, with Tawni, with school. Real men can't be seen studying, Dad says. Tough dudes don't go with black girls. And me – always thinking, why? Why am I in love with a black girl I can't bring home? Why do I want to do good in school?'

'Did you tell your parents?'

'About leaving home or what I think?'

'Both.'

'Neither. Not yet.' Craig sounded sheepish. 'I want to have everything sorted before I say anything. I got a job yesterday, for the holidays, but they said I can have it back in the summer. It's nothing exciting, just runner for the Brady and Lawrence Law Firm, but they like me. I told them I would go to night school and get a degree in political science or law and they said maybe I could intern with them, work for credits, that kind of thing.'

'Will it pay enough?'

'It'll be tight, but hell, my dad lived half his life on

refried beans and he made it. No reason I can't do the same. At least I'll be able to bring Tawni home.'

'You don't really hate him, do you? Your dad, I mean.'

Craig was quiet for a minute. 'My dad busted his butt to get out of the kind of neighbourhood I'm looking for apartments in. He thinks his style is what got him out alive and he wouldn't want his son dishonouring his winning card. He loves me, but I can't be like him. I want to be like me. That's what you should do too, Karen,' he added, when Karen said nothing. 'You should be who you are.'

'I don't know if I want to be like me. I don't know what Mom would say – or Dad.'

'I don't know what Mom and Dad'll do either, but I'm going to do this. It takes guts.'

Karen shook her head.

'Don't let anybody tell you otherwise, Karen. It takes some kind of guts to be honest. Believe me.'

Karen pulled Craig's jacket tighter around her shoulders and looked out the window. Christmas lights were blinking merrily in the early dusk and the street was crowded with shoppers. 'Thing is, I just *have* to see her again, Craig,' she said slowly. 'The feeling's so strong. Makes me feel I'd risk anything. The only place on earth I feel right is next to Allison.'

'Sounds like the real thing, Karen.'

Karen looked into Craig's beautiful, brown eyes. 'Do you have a quarter?'

'In my jacket.' Craig smiled. 'Go ahead. I'll wait. Then I can drive you over.'

'I don't know if she'll want to –' Karen began.

'Try,' Craig cut her off. He leaned across her and opened the door. 'Go on.'

Karen slipped her arms into the sleeves of Craig's jacket, felt in his pocket for some coins and got out of the car. There was a phone booth just to the left of the police station. Karen walked over and went inside.

7

'THANK HEAVENS YOU'RE ALL RIGHT, KAREN,' Allison's mother said, pulling Karen into the house. 'We've been so worried. Thank you,' she yelled in the direction of Craig's car.

Craig honked once and drove off as Allison's mother put her arm around Karen's shoulder and shut the front door. Allison was standing by the living-room couch, looking thin and pale in a black sweatsuit. Her lips trembled when she smiled.

'Your mother called, so upset, wondering if we'd seen you and –'

'Does she know I'm here now? Or anything else?' Karen stopped in her tracks.

'She knows you're here ... but nothing else,' Allison's mother hastened to reassure her. 'I called her after you called. I couldn't bear the thought of her sitting at home, nearly hysterical with worry. But I told her not to come,' she added, as Karen half-turned to leave. 'I told her you needed to work things out with Allison, and that you'd call as soon as you felt up to it. All right?'

Karen nodded, and let Allison's mother lead her to the couch and sit her down.

'I'm going to be in the study helping Berry with his article, if you want me.' She patted Allison lightly on the shoulder and walked off down the hall.

Allison stood rigidly at the side of the couch, hugging her body and chewing her lip.

When the study door closed, Karen stood up. She breathed deeply, trying to sort out the jumbled mess in her brain, to decide what to say, how to say it and what it was she felt. 'Allison,' Karen said, her voice hoarse.

Allison cocked her head slightly and gave a wobbly smile.

'Oh, Allison, I love you,' Karen sobbed, wanting to throw her arms around Allison but unable to move. 'I always have, from the very first day, but I was afraid of what it meant. Oh, Allison, I'm so scared!'

She didn't need to move. One step and Allison was before her, putting her arms around her and hugging her close as Karen sobbed into her hair. 'I love you, too,' Allison said, stroking Karen's back. 'I did from the first day.'

'You don't feel scared, or anything?'

Allison shrugged. 'A little,' she admitted. 'But I feel a whole lot better now than I have for the past two weeks.'

'I was so mean, Allison, I'm sorry. I guess I thought if I didn't see you this would all go away.'

'That's what Mom said.' Allison sat down next to Karen.

'You told your mom!'

'You know we talk.'

'What does she think? And your dad?'

'Mom's funny. She doesn't think anything, really. She says she wants me to enjoy college and find the direction my life should take, the job I want to have ... like my being gay is just a minor detail or something.'

'And your dad?'

'Dad's different. He doesn't think it's anything wrong but he says he's sad a little because he thinks life will be harder for me this way.'

'My mom's not going to think either of those things.'

'What will she say?'

'I don't know, but she's not the only one I'm worried about.'

'Grandma?' Allison smiled.

'I'll know what she thinks when I tell Mom.' Karen was in no mood for humour. 'It's everybody else – Dad, Danny, the others at school, our teachers.'

'Wait a minute, Karen, don't get carried away! We won't be walking around with signs on our backs saying,

"I'm gay!" I'm not going to make an announcement over the PA system.'

'But they'll find out, sooner or later. If you forget and kiss me, or something.' A pleasant warmth flushed Karen's face at the thought. She shook it away in order to remain serious about the problem at hand.

'Maybe you'll be the one to forget,' said Allison quietly.

Karen allowed herself to brush Allison's hair back off her face. 'Maybe I'll be the one,' she agreed.

'I guess it's going to be a new life.' Colour was coming back to Allison's cheeks, as if the prospect of adventure cheered her. 'We won't know exactly how to live it, I suppose, what to say, who to say it to, but if we just try to be honest with ourselves and the people we care about, we'll probably be okay.'

'I don't want people to hate me, or think I'm gross.'

'Some will. But some won't. Maybe it won't be easy but I don't know any other way. This is how I am ... how we are ... and I don't want to think about it too much. I'm kind of hoping Mom's right, that if I just go to school and try to get on with my friends and enjoy my life it won't matter what I am in the end.'

Her confident smile lifted Karen's spirits. 'I love you, Allison,' Karen said, smiling widely. 'And I'm starving.'

'Silly goose!' Allison took Karen's hand and together they went to the kitchen.

Two mugs of steaming hot chocolate were sitting on

the table, on either side of a platter of hot blueberry tarts.

'Dad must have heard us,' Allison said lovingly. 'He's the one that would think of something like this.'

Gratefully, Karen sat down at the table, wrapped her fingers around the mug and carefully sipped her hot chocolate.

'Don't you think you ought to call your mom?'

Karen put the mug down.

'It's too bad you have to deal with her right away but she was worried sick, Karen. It isn't right to let her sit at home like that.'

Karen stared down into her mug without responding.

'She loves you, Karen. Very much, you know that. Be brave.'

'Everybody around me is sure into bravery these days,' Karen muttered.

'What do you mean?'

'Oh, nothing. Just that Craig said I had to be brave, like him, and you said it.'

'I don't know what else to call it. We're going to have to be strong and decide how we feel about everything without allowing our upbringing or friends or society to influence us.'

'If that's possible,' Allison's father said from the doorway.

Karen turned in surprise.

'Sorry,' Berry said. 'I was thirsty.' He walked to the sink

and turned on the cold water. 'All of us are influenced by so many things I don't think there is such a thing as a purely personal opinion. It's hard to come by, anyway.'

'But you weren't raised the way you've raised me,' Allison said, as he leaned over the sink and drank straight from the faucet.

'No, I wasn't.' Berry wiped his mouth and shut off the water. 'Your mother and I do see things differently, and there are others like us, but plenty of people don't. I'm just saying you'll have to understand it's going to be hard for some to accept you.'

'I'm sure we'll find people who will.'

'I'm sure you will too, Alli.'

'It'll be those people who think with their own head,' Karen said quietly. 'That's what Craig said he was trying to do.' She looked at Allison. 'I wasn't sure what he meant.'

'I suppose he means trying to be rational about issues, reflective, not reactive.'

'Don't talk journalese, Daddy.'

'Sorry.' Berry walked back to the doorway. 'Like I said, it's hard to do, but the world would be a better place if we all could.'

'So? Will you call your mom?' Allison said as her father walked out of the kitchen.

Karen nodded.

'Tell her I'll drive you home,' Berry called from the hall.

‘Do you want me to come with you?’ Allison reached across the table and took Karen’s hand.

‘No, no, I better go alone. I don’t have a clue what to say.’ She looked beseechingly at Allison.

‘Don’t try to plan it. Just say what comes out. It’s easier.’

As Karen stepped out of Berry’s car, bundled up in Allison’s ski jacket, she almost wished it were all a dream. She barely had a chance to thank Allison’s father for driving her home when the front door to her house was thrown open and her mother practically flew down the steps, her blue robe billowing out behind her.

‘Karen! Karen!’ she cried, seizing her and hugging her breath away. ‘I was so worried!’ She held Karen out at arm’s length and started to cry.

‘Let’s go into the house, Mom,’ Karen said uncomfortably. Arm-in-arm they walked back to the house as Karen’s mother pulled a wad of tissues from her pocket and blew her nose.

‘I couldn’t imagine where you could have gone. Your purse is here, and your keys ... and hour after hour not a sign ...’ Karen’s mother pressed the tissue against her mouth between sentences as if trying to trap the sobs before they escaped.

'I'm sorry I worried you.' Karen took Allison's jacket off and walked wearily to the kitchen. 'I didn't mean to.'

'Worried?' Her mother followed her in. 'I was hysterical by evening. If Candice hadn't called saying you phoned Allison I would have called the police!'

'I've been having a hard time lately.' Karen fidgeted with the tablecloth.

'Look, here ... sit down. Are you hungry? I'll make some soup and we'll talk.' Mom began to bustle about.

'Mom.' Karen took her mother's hands and pulled her slightly to force her to look into her face. 'I don't want soup. I lied to you about Allison.'

'Something's wrong, isn't it?' Her mother paled, pulled away from Karen and sat down at the table. 'Let's talk about it,' she said, smiling unconvincingly.

'Mom, I'm gay.' Karen was still standing. 'I've been fighting with myself for a while but I don't want to struggle anymore. I'm gay and I'm in love with Allison.'

Her mother opened her mouth, then closed it. She opened her hands, palms up toward Karen in a mute plea, then balled them into fists on the tabletop. 'Are you sure?'

Karen almost laughed. 'I wouldn't be going through all this if I wasn't.'

'What makes you think you're ... gay? Who in the world put such a silly idea in your head? My daughter could never ...'

'Mom.' Karen sat down and reached for her, but her

mother pulled her hands away.

'You aren't old enough to know things like that, to make these kinds of choices ...'

'I'm not making a choice, I just am.'

'To hell!' Mom shouted, startling them both. She pushed away from the table and started pacing the kitchen. 'I won't have you doing something so ridiculous! I did not fight to keep this family together after your father and I divorced to have you go on some silly adolescent whim and ruin everything I planned for you.' The tears came again, defying the wad of tissues she held to stem their flow.

'I'm still me, Mom.' Karen felt a child-like fear inside. Mom refused to look at her. 'I'm the same Karen,' she persisted, 'trying to be a good student and a good daughter. I'm not any different.'

Mom turned and stared at her. 'Not any different? It's totally unnatural – against nature, against God!'

Allison, meet Grandma, Karen thought. 'I can't help it, Mom. I didn't want to be this way, I just am.' She could feel herself starting to cry and tried to delay it by digging her nails into the palms of her hands. 'I've known for a while that I wasn't ... like everybody else, like most other girls, but I tried to ignore it, to fight it, pretend it wasn't there. It was making me go crazy.'

Mom looked away without responding.

'You saw how I've been these last couple of weeks, going bananas all because I refused to believe it, to accept it.'

'Did Allison convince you of all this?' Still Mom kept her face averted.

'No! She didn't know either. We just ... it just happened.'

Mom winced involuntarily and her shoulders shook slightly. 'Why? Why do you want to do this now, now that things have gotten so good, now that I was actually feeling happy?'

'I didn't mean to, Mom.' There was no stopping the flood now. 'I don't want to make you sad,' Karen cried. 'I tried not to tell you. I love you, Mom. Please. Please, I want you to still love me. Can't you still love me?' She covered her face with her hands and sobbed.

'I still love you,' Mom said, kneeling down by the chair and hugging Karen. 'I still love you.'

They cried that way for a while, holding on to each other. Mom released Karen first, and stood up fumbling in her pocket for more tissues. Karen watched her every move as she blew her nose, wiped her eyes and walked slowly to the pantry.

'You may not want soup but I do.' Mom pulled out a can and bent down to get a saucepan.

Karen watched her open the can, pour the contents into the pot and put it over the flame.

'What do you want me to do?' Mom asked, her back to Karen.

'Do? Nothing. What do you mean?' Karen knew her

face was a mess but she had no tissues. Gingerly she pulled up the edge of the tablecloth and wiped her nose and eyes.

'How am I supposed to act, what am I supposed to say about this ... this information?' There was no sarcasm or irony in Mom's voice. She suddenly looked small and frail to Karen, standing at the stove in her favourite robe and slippers.

Karen went to her and put her arms around her from behind, leaning her face against her shoulder. 'You don't have to do anything. Nothing's really different, you'll see,' she added when her mother's body tensed beneath her touch. 'I'm not going to do anything wild, go on TV or tell all my friends. I'm just going to act normal, be like I've always been.'

'Except that you'll be in love with Allison.'

'Except that.' Karen released her mother and came to the side of the stove so that she could see her face. 'But I'll still do well in school and go out with friends and pick a good college.'

'What about your father? Dear God, how will I face Patrick?' Still holding the soup spoon Mom turned to look at Karen.

Karen shook her head. 'I don't know, Mom. Maybe we can just say nothing. I told *you*. I'm not going to make a public announcement. Dad doesn't have to know.'

Mom looked doubtful. 'Will you still date – see – Craig? Does he know?'

Karen was pleased to see simple curiosity taking over from the sadness. 'He knows. He's a good, good friend.'

Her mother nodded. 'Do I tell my colleagues? What do I tell Albert?'

'Who's Albert, Mom?'

Mom's cheeks flushed a little and she blew her nose once more before answering. 'Albert? He's a man I've been seeing, I guess you'd say, for lunch, at the office. We work together and I ...'

'You like him,' Karen encouraged her.

Mom nodded. 'He's a very nice man, a hard worker, an honest, decent person who –'

'Grandma's not listening, Mom. I'm sure he's a great guy.'

Mom smiled and shook herself. 'It's so hard to be free of strong opinions, even if you're not convinced you share them.'

Karen was genuinely impressed with her mother's effort. 'I'm really glad to hear you say that.'

Her mother took the pot off the stove and poured its contents into a bowl.

'You know what Craig said when I told him?' Karen continued after Mom got a spoon and sat down to eat her soup. 'He said he was trying to think about things with his own head. That's why he's still my friend.'

Her mother shook her head. 'It's not always that easy. Sometimes a person doesn't know how she thinks.'

'I know.' Karen sat down beside her and broke off a piece of bread. 'But it's got to be good to try.'

'What do I tell Albert?'

'I don't know, whatever you want.'

'Albert suggested you were having some typical teen-year problems and that I should just let you work them out without pushing you, but I doubt he dreamed something like this could be happening.'

Karen sighed deeply. 'I hope he likes you enough to stay if you tell him, but you don't have to, if you don't want to. I'm not going to give you away, or anything.'

'Life goes on,' Mom sighed, 'full of surprises and situations I haven't a clue how to handle.'

'We'll learn how,' Karen said, pulling her chair closer. 'I'll tell you what I find out and you tell me what you find out, okay?'

Mom nodded and smiled reluctantly.

'Can I have some of that soup?' asked Karen.

'Sure. Here, take the rest.'

They sat in the kitchen, trying on their new relationship, talking as two women, two friends, might talk, striving mightily to be more than mother and daughter, more than daughter and grandchild.

'I love you, Mom,' Karen said before going off to bed. Her mother was just rinsing out the bowls they'd used and putting away the spoons.

'I love you, too, Karen,' Mom replied, turning to look

at her daughter standing in the doorway. 'I don't know exactly what I think about all this, and I'm not sure if things will ever really be the same for us, but I do love you. I'm sure of that.' She smiled briefly, then wiped off the kitchen counter and turned off the light. 'You go on to bed,' she added, pushing Karen gently out of the kitchen. 'I promised Albert I'd call.'

Karen kissed her mother's cheek without a word and went off to her room, feeling a strange mixture of relief and anxiety. She did not know what her future would be like from now on but she decided to simply live as she'd been promising herself that day, taking each moment as fresh, unplanned for and unpredicted. It was the only way she knew how and she prayed it would be enough.

8

MID-TERM EXAMS WENT SPLENDIDLY and Karen thanked her lucky stars that she and Allison had got over the hurdle together. She knew that had she taken them before she would have failed. The last week of school went without a hitch, though Karen was conscious about the way she acted when she and Allison were together, and the Christmas break was welcomed by all. Karen even spent a week with her father and Danny in San Francisco, able to enjoy the city and Dad's guided tours unhindered with worries, even when Dad teased her about Craig. Accepting herself made it easier to weather his ribbing without reacting, and she concentrated on taking what was good and simply getting through what was not. It seemed to be working.

A few days after Christmas, Danny went back to San Francisco and Karen stayed home to prepare for her mother's party. Having Allison with her to cook and shop and decorate had her feeling as carefree and joyous as a child, and she had to keep reminding herself not to kiss Allison or hug her in her mother's presence.

Mom seemed to be making a valiant effort to be non-judgemental, treating Allison as warmly as she always had and going ahead with her plans for the Christmas party. The only thing she couldn't handle was physical contact between them. All Karen had to do was slip once, kiss Allison on the cheek, and she could see her mother go rigid and red, her lips drawing together in a tight, white line. She wouldn't say anything, and the instant would pass, but it was impossible to ignore. Never in her life had Karen done anything to warrant such a reaction and she did her best not to provoke it now.

As the hour for the party drew close, Karen was actually more interested in observing her mother. She changed her outfit three times, and brushed her hair incessantly. She checked and re-checked the effect of their decorations by standing at the living-room door and surveying the room, hand on hip, and then she'd make some minor adjustment to the location of the platters of snack food or the angle of the poinsettia. Even Allison noticed, and she and Karen exchanged knowing glances.

Still, neither was prepared for the way Mom practically jumped out of her skin when the doorbell rang. 'You get it, Karen,' she said, smoothing her dress down in front of the mirror in the hallway. 'Go on, hurry!'

So Karen went to the door and got her first look at Albert. He wasn't anything outstanding and that one instant was all she needed to take him in. Average height, average build, brown hair, brown eyes, clean-shaven. He was holding a red plastic bag and a bottle of champagne, and his hand felt slightly damp when he shook Karen's.

'So you're Karen,' he said, smiling much too widely. 'It's a pleasure to meet you.' He seemed to forget to release her hand and Karen had to pull it away. 'I'm early, probably. It's a habit with me,' he continued as Karen stepped aside and gestured for him to come in. 'My military upbringing.' He was talking now to nobody, as Allison and Mom were still in the living room and Karen was at his back, closing the front door. He turned then and smiled again.

'No, we were expecting you,' Karen said. It was so obvious that he wanted her to like him, to accept him, that her worries about him accepting her faded. In a sense, they were both anxious to please and it almost made her laugh. 'We're in the living room,' she added, and she motioned him to follow her.

'Carol! You look ...' Albert stopped, glanced at Karen, and hastily concluded, 'I brought champagne, and some small presents. Nothing big.'

'Lovely,' said Mom, taking the bottle from him and indicating the Christmas tree in the corner by the bay window. 'Just set the bag there.' And then they both stood where they were, as if not only words but their entire bodies were failing them.

Albert tore his eyes away from her first, and made to go to the tree. 'I didn't know what to get you,' he said to nobody in particular. 'Not having met you and knowing only what your mother ...' Again he stopped, and passed his hand nervously through his hair. A shine of sweat appeared on his forehead.

Karen took pity on him. 'It was very nice of you.' Taking the bag she herself set it under the tree. At that same moment Allison took the champagne from Mom and went to the kitchen with it.

'Well,' Mom said, casting about for something to say. 'Well!' Then she smiled wryly and sat heavily on the couch. 'My goodness. I feel as nervous as a kid,' she burst out. 'This is ridiculous!'

'Me, too,' said Albert, taking out a handkerchief and wiping his face. 'You'd think I was afraid you'd bite.' He looked at Karen, and she wondered suddenly what exactly her mother had told him. 'And you must be Allison,' Albert said, as Allison walked back into the living room. His artificial cheerfulness was giving him away. Obviously, Karen's mother had told him everything.

'I am.' Allison was feeling as uncomfortable as everybody else and when the doorbell rang they all four leaped to their feet to answer it.

It was a group of Mom's colleagues and with their

arrival the tension was broken and the party began. Everyone ate and drank and toasted, played parlour games and improvised carols and forgot, in the cheer of the moment, who they were and what they meant to each other. Everybody said that it was a wonderful Christmas party and it was well past midnight when it started to break up. By one o'clock, only Albert was left.

Karen figured that Mom and Albert would want to be alone for a bit and was happy to say goodnight and leave them, but her mother kept assuring Karen that they'd only be a minute. Just a minute and she, too, would be in her bed. It was as though they had exchanged roles, and Karen took advantage of this new development to do something she never would have done before. She pressed her ear to her door and listened to their conversation.

'Rough start,' Albert said, and the couch creaked when he sat down on it.

'You can say that again.' Mom, too, sat down, most likely right next to him, Karen thought.

'She's a lovely girl, Carol. Seems totally normal.'

'She is normal, Albert.'

'You know what I mean. Come on, Carol. Don't worry. Your daughter behaved beautifully, and so did her friend. The party was a smashing success and I even think she likes me. At least she doesn't dislike me.'

'Patrick doesn't know, Danny ... nobody at work and ...'

'Carol! Don't get ahead of yourself. You act like she has to wear a scarlet letter or something. Everything went wonderfully this evening. Nobody has to know.'

'But it'll come out eventually. She ... I ... we can't hide something this big forever. She might, or somebody might say something ... she even ... they may even kiss and ... I wouldn't have told even you, Albert, except that I couldn't live with the news. And you, be honest, you weren't ... you're not thrilled.'

'I wasn't thrilled mostly because I had no idea how to act, or how she would act, or what people would say when we ...'

He stopped, and Karen imagined from the creaking of the couch that he had shifted position, perhaps he had turned and taken Mom's hand.

'When we're all together,' he concluded. 'It's never easy to step into a readymade family – in the best of circumstances the kids could hate you, or the ex could kill you! Just kidding, Carol,' his voice was muffled by the sound of Karen's mother moving, probably getting quickly to her feet. 'Come here. I'm trying to inject a note of humour into this deadly conversation.'

'You're not funny!' were the words, but her voice said something sweeter.

'I know. Listen, Carol, I asked you to marry me and you said yes. I asked you before I knew and I asked you after. I'm telling you again now. I love you and I want to marry you. I don't have the foggiest idea what to tell Patrick, what or when to tell Danny, whether we should say anything at all in the office. All I know is that she's a fine girl and that none of this is going to be easy. But mostly I know I want to be with you and have you all as my family, whatever happens.'

Karen could hear Mom sigh, and then she could hear them kiss, and then she felt guilty for listening. Tip-toeing away from the door she got quietly into bed, still fully dressed. She lay there, feeling the funny mix of anxiety and relief that seemed to be her perpetual state these days. On the one hand she was relieved that Albert was going to try to make a go of things despite everything. She was a bit annoyed that her mother would have agreed to marry a man without so much as mentioning a word to her, but she realised at the same time that with the way things had been going lately it was no surprise that her mother just kept things to herself. And Albert was a nice man. Ordinary, but brave too. There really were a lot of things to worry about. Still, the party had been wonderful, and nobody knew anything was afoot. The same could be said of school, of her trip to her father's. Nobody was any the wiser and she could relax and try to enjoy her senior year the way Allison said she was going to. Albert was right. She did not, in fact, have to wear a scarlet letter. It was probably all going to be much easier than she'd anticipated.

Karen lived with this conviction the rest of the Christmas holidays but it took just one day back at school to rip her certainty to shreds. The day hadn't even started. Karen was just walking up to her locker when she saw the words on it, done in black marker in big bold letters. KAREN IS A LEZ. The sight froze her, left her gasping like a fish out of water, as if somebody had just punched the air out of her lungs. The furtive glances of those around her galvanised her into action, however, and she already had a marker of her own out of her bag before she'd made it to her locker, and was frantically covering over the horrible words when she heard Allison's voice behind her.

'Hey, Karen! How's being back –' she stopped in mid-sentence when Karen turned to look at her, her face almost wild with anger and shame. She had already covered up most of the offending words but Allison didn't need to see them to guess. 'Somebody wrote something nasty.'

'That's right,' Karen said through clenched teeth. 'And I bet I know who.'

'Robbie.'

Karen didn't need to answer.

'This is called harassment and all we have to do is go to the principal and ...'

Again, the look on Karen's face stopped Allison mid-sentence.

Allison could see the struggle, could tell that Karen was trying mightily not to turn on her in anger. 'I didn't say it would be easy,' Allison said softly, afraid now to even look into Karen's eyes.

Karen turned back to her locker and finished covering up the words. There was now a huge black blotch right across the face of it, marking her as surely as a scarlet letter would. 'I know,' Karen finally said, rapidly turning the lock and opening the door. She threw her books inside and looked again at Allison. 'I know. It'll be okay. Must be how he gets his kicks.'

'So we'll try to just ignore him?'

Karen nodded. 'We'll try. But I have an awful feeling we're going to have to face friend and foe alike much sooner than we thought.'

The foe came on cue. Karen had barely got the sentence out when Robbie came sauntering down the corridor flanked by two of his buddies. They were dressed identically, all three in soft, expensive leather, and they all three had their baseball caps turned backwards on their heads. There were lots of other students going down the corridor, as well as teachers and coaches and office personnel, but to Karen it was as if nobody was there but herself and Robbie. She knew that what she ought to do was simply ignore him. Just turn around and get her things out of her locker, or even take

Allison's arm and head off in the opposite direction, but something in his leering smile froze her legs and she couldn't seem to react any other way but to stand there dumbly and watch him walk by.

'Game ain't over yet,' Robbie said as he walked by her, so softly that Karen wasn't even sure she'd heard right. And then he was gone, up the stairs to his first class.

'Creep!' Allison was flushed and angry but definitely not cowed. 'Everybody knows he's just a bully, Karen. He'll be easy to ignore.'

But Karen felt neither anger nor defiance. Something cold and heavy weighed her down. Dread.

That entire morning, Karen interpreted every glance, every whisper, every smile in her direction as a sure sign that Robbie was spreading the news. By lunchtime she was so despondent that Allison got angry.

'For goodness sake, Karen. Stop it! Nobody said a word, did they?'

'That doesn't mean ...'

'Yes it does! You are determined to believe that Robbie is going around telling the whole school that we're gay and –'

'That *I'm* gay,' Karen interrupted morosely.

'Whatever! When probably he just wants to bully you and hasn't said a thing to anybody. Nobody's behaving any different with me. You're imagining the worst. Just cut it out. That's what he wants, you know. He wants to get to you and it sure didn't take much. You've got to have a stronger backbone than this!'

They were eating lunch in the library, alone at a back table by the reference books, and rain was pouring down the windows, doing nothing to raise Karen's spirits. 'I'm not ready to have to deal with this,' Karen said, trying to keep her voice down though she felt like yelling.

'So far, there is nothing to deal with but your own paranoia!'

Karen raised her eyebrows. Allison could be quite prickly when she finally got mad. In a way, it made Karen happy. She didn't want to be the only one with a temper. 'I am not paranoid,' she said, but she had started to smile and Allison didn't miss it.

'Okay. So stop worrying so much. Denise and Roger wanted to know if we'd like to join them for that history project – remember, the research on the Nazi rise to power. I said we would. Okay?'

The last thing Karen wanted to read about was Nazis but the paper was due in three weeks and, since it was supposed to be a group effort, she had to join somebody sometime. 'Okay. When will we get together to plan?'

'Roger has theatre this afternoon so we said tomorrow. My house at four-thirty. I'll have Dad make some brownies. It'll be fun.'

Karen marvelled how easily Allison could put all worry behind her and get excited over a silly class project and a batch of brownies, but she had to admit that it was better than grimly wondering if the whole school knew she was gay. 'Sounds good,' she said, as enthusiastically as possible. 'Might as well take advantage of being here now and check some books out on the subject.'

'You're right. Good for you. Let's go through the card catalogue.'

And so saying the two girls threw out their empty bags and dug up notepads and pencils, ready to launch themselves back into their normal routine of school, studies and friends.

Sitting with the library books at the kitchen table late that afternoon, Karen had almost forgotten the inauspicious beginning to her last semester in school when she heard Danny come banging through the front door and stomping into the kitchen. She looked up as he loomed in the doorway, and gasped.

Danny's shirt was torn and dirty, and specks of blood were scattered across the front of it like a gory design. His face was bruised and swollen and he had a fat lip. 'You ought to see the other guy,' Danny said heavily before she'd had a chance to ask him what had happened.

Karen stared at him as though he were speaking a foreign language.

Danny went to the freezer and took out a bag of ice, placing it gingerly on his split lip. Then he sat down at the table. 'Dad's going to flip when he hears about this, but at least I taught that bozo to watch his mouth – when I'm around anyway.'

'What in the world ...'

'And cut that innocent look, would you? As if you didn't know some creep called Robbie is telling everybody in Seaworth that you're a lesbian. I mean, you sure don't do anything to make people think otherwise but to actually say it to me! Like I'd just sit there and take it. He really miscalculated that one!'

The impact of what Danny was saying didn't so much hit Karen as slowly strangle her. She felt like she was choking, as if her tongue had blocked her windpipe, making it impossible for her to speak or breathe.

'Thank you, Danny. Thank you for standing up for me,' Danny said sarcastically. 'Some appreciation might be in order, don't you think?'

'Danny ... I don't know what to say,' Karen finally managed to blurt out. 'You shouldn't care what he says, you shouldn't get in fights ...'

'Over you? Well, I, for one, care what people say about our family. And so should you. At least enough to act normal – you know, see Craig more than once a month, for instance, try to say goodbye to Allison without looking like you'll never see her again.'

A powerful wave of shame swept over Karen as she realised that her feelings were open and naked for all to see.

'I mean, I'm not going to be the gladiator your whole life, you know,' Danny was saying, truly feeling like he deserved more gratitude than he was getting.

'I don't need a gladiator. And I'll see who I want, when I want.' A slow-burning anger was taking over, welling up from the pit of her stomach.

'You're really selfish, you know that? You don't care what Mom or Dad or I feel like when we hear people say things about you. It's not very –'

'You'd better get used to it.' Karen had risen from the table and she stood facing her brother, trembling from fury. 'I don't exist in order to make you look good. I'm who I am, like it or not.' Something inside warned Karen that she should stop right now, leave the kitchen, go for a walk, but the anger was too strong, fed by the righteous expression on Danny's face.

'Hanging around with Allison has warped your mind,' Danny said flippantly as he walked over to the sink and turned on the faucet. He poured soap into his hands and gingerly began to wash his bruised face. 'Anyhow, you do what you want. As for me, nobody, but nobody's going to get away with garbage like that,' he spluttered as he rinsed.

'Even if it's true?' Karen's voice was low and menacing, and it had the same effect on Danny as the warning growl of an attacking dog.

Danny turned slowly from the sink, the water still running, his face dripping onto the floor. He stared at her with his mouth half-open, contorted into a grimace of disgust.

'You're going to spend your whole life in fights,' Karen informed him.

The implication of her words was too much for Danny. 'You mean it's true?' He practically choked on the words, looking almost as though he would vomit.

'All of it. What are you going to do about that, big boy?'

For a moment, Danny couldn't speak, and during the seconds that followed Karen could see the different emotions playing themselves out on his face – he was sickened, frightened, furious. He wanted to speak but nothing came out. He wanted to hit her but stood where he was, his neck muscles bulging and his breath coming rapid and shallow as though he'd just run a marathon. 'You make me sick!' he finally spat out, and tears sprang to his eyes. 'You *are* sick!' He was about to cry and grabbed a towel before charging past her and out of the kitchen.

The tap was still running but Karen felt too heavy and worn to go turn it off.

'Danny, what on earth?' Mom had just walked in the front door, and at the sound of her voice Karen slumped back down into her chair and dropped her head onto her arms on the kitchen table.

'This family is sick! Sick!' Danny screamed at Mom in

the hallway. 'I'm moving out. I'm going to Dad's. Don't you touch me!'

Tears rose against the back of Karen's eyelids and seeped out from the sides.

'Danny, calm down,' said Mom. 'What is going on here?!'

'Go ask Karen! Go ask your sweet, dyky daughter!'

Karen's mother gasped and Karen rocked slowly in her chair, trying to keep from wailing like a child.

The phone rang. Karen sat where she was. Danny ran off and slammed the door of his bedroom. 'Hello?' Mom sounded weak and breathless. 'Oh, Albert!' Now she too was crying, and Karen knew, after she had put the phone down without uttering another word, that Albert was on his way.

In the time it took for Albert to arrive they had each claimed a section of the house and stayed there – Karen in the kitchen, Danny in his bedroom, and Mom sitting on the living-room couch. By the time the doorbell rang Karen had a splitting headache. It was the only part of her that felt alive. The rest of her body was wood.

Karen could hear Albert and her mother have a conference in low voices, and then Mom went and knocked on Danny's door and Albert walked into the kitchen. His face looked a bit ashen and his smile was tight and sheepish.

'Hi, Karen. Mind if I sit?' He gestured to a kitchen chair and sat when Karen did not respond. 'Look, I don't know how you feel about me coming in here – butting in, you probably think – but me and your mother ...'

'I know.' Karen was in no mood for heart-to-heart conversation. 'You're getting married so you have a right.'

'A right – no,' spluttered Albert. 'Not a right. An interest, you could say, or desire to ...'

'Whatever. It doesn't matter. You can't do any good. Nothing's going to be any good. Not ever again.' Karen struggled against the tears. Her head was pounding mercilessly and she couldn't bear the hurt expression on Albert's face.

'Listen. I've never been a father before. I am totally out of my depth here but I care about your mother and I care about you and Danny. I can't bear seeing Carol like this. If we're going to be a family we'll have to work this out. It's not that terrible.'

'No? Danny hates me. Everybody in school knows I'm gay. Dad'll kill me.'

'Danny can't hate you. You're his sister and that's that.'

Karen snorted.

'It'll be hard for him,' Albert continued nonetheless, 'it might take a while but he'll come round. And your Dad won't kill anybody. Karen, we'll face all this together, okay? I know it doesn't seem like much but I don't know what else to offer. We'll handle it a step at a time, together.'

Albert reached over and gently patted Karen's arm, and though she did not reply or respond in any way, he knew she would not reject him.

'I can't get Danny to come out of his room.' Mom walked into the kitchen and joined them at the table. Her eyes were red and swollen and she had her trusty tissue balled in her hand. 'Oh, Karen, couldn't you have waited? A better time, a better way?'

'I didn't mean to. Besides, it's all over school. This guy, Robbie, he's telling everybody.'

'You couldn't have denied it?'

'It's too late for that now, Carol,' Albert answered for her. 'It wouldn't make any difference at this point. But we shouldn't get carried away. Rumours pass. People will forget and things will go back to normal.'

Neither Mom nor Karen believed him, but he insisted anyway.

'Oh, things will probably be hairy for a while. I know it's going to be extra hard for you, Karen, but I promise, it'll wind down and pretty soon nobody will mention it again.'

'That's probably true about school, Albert, but the bigger problem is right here at home. Danny ... Patrick ...'

Albert knew she was right but refused to concede defeat. 'Only a beast would forsake his own daughter. And Danny will just have to get used to it.'

'Maybe it'll pass,' Mom said suddenly, looking into Karen's face. 'Maybe it's a stage, something you think is true but isn't really, and you'll see in a while that what you really feel –' The look on Karen's face stopped her. 'Just when I thought things had become good,' Mom murmured then, looking away.

'Well, the way I see it we have two choices. Either we sit and stew and wring our hands over this or we put it behind us, roll up our sleeves and keep on living, come what may!' Albert's voice was forcibly cheerful and his heartiness fake, but Karen realised that what he said was true. Nobody could do a thing to change what had happened. All they could do was keep going.

9

THE FIRST HURDLE OF MAJOR SIGNIFICANCE WAS, as they expected, Karen's father. Danny wasted no time and called him that very evening; the next Saturday, Dad was at their door by nine in the morning. He hadn't called to say he was coming, and Danny never said a word, so Karen was totally unprepared when she woke up and found him in the kitchen. It was obvious from her mother's strained expression and her father's open shirt-collar that they were well into an argument when Karen walked in, but they both held their tongues when she appeared in the doorway, each waiting for the other to say something first.

Karen had no time to prepare her defence or steel herself for the onslaught and could not think of one word of resistance when her father mapped out his decision.

'First thing we'll do is get you some serious help,' he

said – no Hello, Good morning or How are you. 'I've got medical coverage but it doesn't pay for psychiatrists, so we're going to have to shell out for this ourselves. But we will. Starting Monday. I made an appointment for you with a man a friend of mine in San Francisco recommended. You'll see him once a week. You'll stop seeing Allison for good.'

'Patrick, you can't come in here and –'

'And you!' Dad whirled around and practically spat at Mom. 'You have failed completely to raise the children properly. You should be getting help as well!'

'There is nothing I did to cause this!'

'It's not normal and it never would have happened if you hadn't left me!'

'Just because you can't accept a daughter who's –'

'No daughter of mine is ...' he broke in, but he was unable to finish the sentence.

'Daddy,' Karen couldn't bear to have them fight.

He stopped and turned to her. 'Listen, Karen. I'm sure that you can overcome this problem with the right kind of help and I'm going to provide it. You just do what the doctor says.'

'Maybe your father's right, Karen.' Karen stared at her mother in mute despair as Mom sat down slowly in front of her. 'Maybe going to a psychiatrist is the answer.'

Karen shook her head but couldn't find the words to go with her feelings.

'It takes the father of a household to put sense into everybody,' Dad said with satisfaction. 'I'm sure this is just some malarkey that girl put into your head. I don't want you seeing her anymore, understand?'

Again, Karen could only shake her head. She felt as though somebody had slipped an erase procedure into her brain. It was as if she couldn't put her thoughts together, couldn't explain what she felt, couldn't even remember how to say two simple words.

To her father, her silence meant agreement. He pulled a cheque book out of his back pocket. 'Listen, I've got a plane to catch. Here's five hundred dollars. That should cover the initial sessions.' He scribbled his signature, ripped the cheque out and handed it to Mom.

Mom wasn't saying anything either. And she wouldn't take the cheque. She sat with her hands on her lap, looking at him with a blank expression on her face.

Dad huffed, then set the cheque down in the middle of the table. 'I'll try to make it back in a couple of weeks – three maybe – we're at a critical stage. And you can tell me how much better everything's getting, okay, darling?' He bent over and kissed Karen quickly on the cheek. Glancing once at his ex-wife he patted Karen on the shoulder and then walked out of the kitchen.

'Want some company, Dad?' Karen heard Danny ask. He had been waiting in the living room

'Yes, son.'

In the couple of minutes that followed, while Danny got his jacket and their father called a cab, Karen and her mother sat without moving at the kitchen table, Karen staring listlessly into space, her mother concentrating on her hands neatly folded in her lap.

'See you all soon!' Dad shouted from the front door. And then they were gone.

Karen looked over at her mother and found that she was staring over into her own face.

'I just can't do it anymore,' Mom said before Karen could speak. 'I just can't.' She wasn't about to cry, nor was there anger in her words. Just a heaviness that matched the bottomless pit in Karen's heart.

'What, Mom?'

'Make things right. Keep everybody happy.'

'Mom, I don't want to go to a psychiatrist. And I'm not going to stop seeing Allison.' She sounded more adamant than she felt, and tempered the effect so as not to appear impertinent. 'I mean, we share almost all our classes, we've got a history project together, and she's my best friend.'

Mom shook her head. 'You don't have to do anything you don't want to. You turn eighteen in just two months, Karen. Neither your father nor I can force you. And frankly, I'm too weary to try.'

Karen didn't know what to make of this. It wasn't as though her mother was trying to convince her of anything but she wasn't defending her either. It was as if she were abdicating altogether, giving up. A deep fear caught at Karen's breathing. 'Do you still love me?'

Mom pushed the chair away from the table and stood up, slowly pulling her hair back from her face. She dropped her arms limply by her sides. 'I still love you.'

And then she walked out of the kitchen and into her room, closing the door behind her.

Karen sat still, noticing the heavy rain clouds passing by her window as the wind cleared the weather. Almost eighteen. She had been looking forward to the big day but realised now that she hadn't really considered what it meant. An adult. Her decisions were now on par with those of her parents, at least legally. Her father couldn't force her to go to the psychiatrist. She could see Allison all she wanted. And yet, the idea did not bring relief. Because it also meant she was on her own. Her father could still make life difficult and having a mother who didn't intend to act like one anymore was frightening. Would Mom no longer be the buffer between Karen and her father? Would she just let Danny act like the horrible brother he was? Were there to be no more Rice Krispie crunchies to help her through the sad times?

Karen was amazed to find tears welling up in her eyes at the memory of her mother cooking up a batch of crunchies with Rice Krispies and marshmallows the day a girl at school had knocked out her two front teeth. It was second grade, and though the teeth had been loose Karen felt sure she would have the ugly hole in her smile for the rest of her life.

But her mother had told her to nibble the crunchies at the side of her mouth, and had assured her that they would indeed grow back, that she was always, but always, a wonderful, beautiful girl.

Still, she was beginning to understand what her mother was feeling. Mom had always been able, through plain determination and with the force of her love, to make things right for everybody. But it was just getting too hard to do that now. As long as it's little things like loose teeth, Karen thought, but when life starts getting this complicated ...

It was an older girl who left the kitchen that Saturday morning, older and heavier with the sense of responsibility, for herself and for her life. Nothing had changed dramatically but Karen felt that she'd stepped through a doorway into another room, and the door to her childhood had closed and locked her out. The weeks that followed were marked by good days and bad days, with the bad predominating in the beginning and tapering down as time went by. Danny refused to speak to Karen at all. He spoke to no one at first, even staying home from school for a few days after their big confrontation. Later he went through the motions, got up for breakfast, went to his classes and basketball practice, talked to his father on the phone every chance he got, but he spent as little time as possible at home and refused to discuss his feelings.

Karen didn't really need to talk to him to know what he had decided to do. He was going to pretend that he did not have a sister, that they weren't related. When they chanced to pass in the school halls he looked right through her, and some of Karen's friends said he even made jokes about her with his teammates. The worst was when Karen saw him exchange the 'brotherly greeting' with Robbie, as if he were a member of his gang. She watched from a distance as they talked, seeing in their posturing a meeting of minds. She often saw him chatting girls up, too, outside the gym or on the lawn in front of the school, but he never brought anybody home.

Karen did not try to talk to him, and she said nothing about seeing him with Robbie. She had enough trouble to deal with. Robbie's handiwork had brought the best and worst out in people and Karen was still reeling from the speed with which some friends just dumped her. One day they'd be smiling and waving in the hallways and the next day she might as well have been invisible. Not everybody did, of course, and in a slow and painful process Karen built a circle around her made up of people she knew liked her the way she was. There was Denise and her boyfriend, Roger, Angela from her English class and Sherry in math. And then there were the kids who didn't seem to care one way or another. They nodded their greetings and mentioned the weather but were neither closer nor more distant once the news got out.

She was developing a tougher skin, too. The first time a girl from the cheerleading squad stared at Karen with open hostility and actually growled 'Dyke' as Karen passed, Karen was too astounded to say a word and was hurt to the core of her being, but she began to learn who to avoid and how to get by. Best of all, Albert had been right. Over time, the novelty faded and nobody seemed to care what she was. The people who rejected her first stayed away, but outright hostility became a rarity as the school year progressed and everybody became entangled in their own problems and concerns. Robbie didn't let up, but even that was starting to seem old, and Karen had actually laughed at the last provocation – a page torn out of a pornographic magazine graphically depicting two women in a sexual act which he had slipped into her locker. He'd written her name and Allison's over the heads of the two women and Karen could even comment that the pretty one was Allison.

Things at home were infinitely more difficult. Having a tight-lipped stranger instead of a brother was hard enough, but it was the calls from her father that really put Karen to the test. He'd called that Monday night, furious that Karen had not kept her appointment with the psychiatrist. Karen had been unlucky enough to answer the phone herself but as he wasn't in the room it was easier for her to defend herself and they argued angrily for a good half-hour before he finally slammed the phone down. His subsequent calls were like clockwork, every other day sometime before eight, but the results were always the same and were beginning to wear Karen down.

True to her word, Mom stopped being peace-maker and buffer and curer-of-all-ills. Their dinners were often completed in total silence and she made no effort to reconcile Danny to the current state of affairs. When Albert came over she did not attempt to keep their little group together. Karen was beginning to like Albert's simple decency, but Danny was deaf to any overture on Albert's part and never took part in their evening conversations. Karen's mother actually took to leaving Danny notes on his bedroom door in lieu of personal communication.

Karen credited Albert with helping to keep her sane. Though it was always with a bit of reticence and his now famous, sheepish smile, Albert never hesitated to ask Karen what she thought of things, how she was feeling, how her friends were taking her and what she thought of them. He didn't ask out of duty, nor as a mouthpiece for her mother. He seemed to truly want to know, to understand, and Karen grew to greatly appreciate the time he spent with her, encouraging her to reflect out loud on the unusual turn her life had taken. He neither supported nor condemned her views but tried to make sense of them in the light of his own knowledge.

Sometimes Karen felt that time was running out, that something big was just out of sight, something awful that would smash into her world and knock it off its shaky foundations. At other times she felt a sense of peace. On the surface, things were under control. She was caught up in school, comfortable with her friends, and keeping her balance at home. Not everything was cheerful, certainly, and there were moments, like the furious conversations with her father, that depressed her, but he was there and she was here and, basically, life went on. Never, though, could Karen have anticipated the complete disaster awaiting her, and it wasn't until afterwards, when Allison told her the whole story, that Karen really comprehended how close she had come to the end.

It had been Allison, in fact, who had set the whole thing in motion. She had asked Karen to wait for her outside the gym after school so that they could take the bus downtown and shop together for an outfit that Allison wanted to buy Karen for her birthday. It was a splendid day in late March, still cold enough to have to wear a sweater but sunny and bright, a light wind keeping the sky clean and the air scented sweetly with perfume from the mimosa trees. Karen waited patiently even though Allison was late, first ten minutes, then twenty, then half an hour. Seaworth High emptied out and by four o'clock Karen was still alone, standing against the sunny western wall of the gymnasium, wondering what had happened. She thought of how Allison had insisted on this outing, how she'd described the red jeans and stripy shirt she'd seen in a small boutique, how good she had said Karen would look in it. Caught up in this reverie she did not hear the footsteps until he grabbed her from behind, pulling her arm up and back to hurt her into submission.

'You're coming with me.' Though she could not turn she didn't have to see him to know it was Robbie.

'Let me go!' Karen tried to pull away but Robbie was fast, strong and cruel. He had dragged her to the back of the building in half a second, threatening to break her aching arm unless she shut up. Once on the other side he slapped her with his other hand, flat across the face, slamming her body back against the chainlink fence. Before Karen could react he hit her again, this time in the stomach, and she was doubled up on the ground when she heard screeching brakes and felt dust in her mouth. Hauling her to her feet Robbie shoved her into the back of his brother's Porsche and got in beside her.

And that was when Allison noticed her, staring out the car window without seeing, blood seeping from the side of her mouth as the Porsche streaked past the library Allison had just left at a run.

Karen had not, in fact, seen Allison. She hadn't seen anything and was only barely conscious of the short exchange between Robbie and two of his friends sitting up front. Karen was trying not to throw up, concerned, despite everything, about ruining the fine leather upholstery. It was as though none of this were happening, so concentrated was she on quelling the cramps in her stomach, and only when the car stopped and the door opened did Karen fully realise what had actually happened. Robbie dragged her out and, without saying a word, pushed her before him, shoving her towards an abandoned-looking building. Any time she slowed down or tried to turn he shoved her from behind, sending her sprawling more than once. Each time he'd pull her roughly to her feet as though she were made of straw, making no sound, saying not a word. It was this lack of his usual banter, the complete silence, that terrified Karen the most. Robbie had gone over the edge. She knew it. And he was taking her with him.

10

ALLISON COULD NOT HAVE STOOD ON THE LAST STEP in front of the library for more than a split second but her recounting of the moment later seemed to encompass an entire day. She could remember every sound, every sight, every puff of wind. The sun was slanting lower in the sky, giving the buildings the almost golden hue of a late spring afternoon, and the wind was growing slightly colder against her face. She had started running before the Porsche had even turned the corner, running with her mouth open and nothing coming out, because she already knew there was nothing she could say or do to stop them. And despite the fact that she ran faster than she'd ever run in her life, despite streaking wildly across people's yards and taking shortcuts over fences, Allison could even remember the names on the mailboxes she passed. When she threw herself against

Karen's door, pounding it with both fists and screaming incoherently, Allison knew that in the minutes it had taken to get there Karen could already be dead.

She practically fell on top of Danny when he opened the door.

'Call the police! The police, hurry!' she screamed, pushing Danny with both hands towards the telephone in the hall. In her total panic she did not see Karen's mother come to the kitchen door, nor her father, standing just a few feet away from Danny.

'Allison! What is it? What happened?' It was Mom who moved first, throwing off her apron and drying her hands on her skirt as she walked briskly toward her.

'The police!' Allison wailed, flailing against Danny in her effort to make it to the phone. He wasn't moving fast enough, dazed as he was by her hysterical behaviour.

'Good Lord, Allison, calm down a moment and tell us what's happening.' Mom had grasped Allison's arm and was trying to turn her so that she could see her face but Allison just kept pushing forward, as if thrashing underwater to get to the telephone.

Dad took two strides, grabbed Allison's shoulders and roughly turned her towards him. 'Calm down, girl.' He shook her slightly, conscious that she didn't even know who he was. 'I'm Karen's father. What's going on?'

Perhaps it was the tone of his voice, or the fact that Allison was effectively immobilised, but she stopped struggling and looked up at him, tears streaming down her face. 'I saw Karen,' she blubbered. 'I saw Karen in Robbie's car, blood on her face. She's been kidnapped! He's taken her! He'll kill her!'

Had she been able to turn around, she would have seen Danny stiffen, but he did not speak.

'Who is Robbie? Are you sure?' Mom was beginning to feel afraid.

'Now try to calm down and explain yourself.' Dad let go of Allison's shoulders and fished a handkerchief out of his pocket. He handed it to her but did not release her from his stern gaze.

Allison knew that every second counted and she was so frightened she could barely speak coherently, but she tried to make them understand that Karen was in terrible danger. 'Robbie is ... is a guy from school, a really ... nasty piece of work,' she stuttered, trying to choke back her sobs. 'He took Karen away in his Porsche!'

'Perhaps the young lad was simply giving her a lift somewhere?' Dad said, trying to sound unworried. 'Or showing off his car?'

'No, no,' Allison shook her head frantically. 'He tried to hurt her once already, once before Christmas, he almost ... he almost raped her!'

Mom gasped and Dad stepped forward again and placed both hands hard on Allison's shoulders.

'What on earth are you saying?' Dad growled, looking

both angry and suspicious.

Mom was starting to feel weak in the knees. 'Karen never told me.'

'Please, please call the police,' Allison begged. 'She didn't say anything because – oh I don't know why but it's true, he did, and I know she'd never go any place with him. Never! He's going to hurt her! I know it.'

Dad looked at Mom, his face stone-hard but his eyes questioning. Mom had no answer to give. Only Danny was able to galvanise them into action.

'I wouldn't put it past him.' He'd said it quietly, but they all heard and turned to look at him. 'I know who he is. And I wouldn't put it past him.'

At that, Mom ran over to the phone and called the police as Allison crumpled again, sobbing out loud like a lost child.

'Allison! Pull yourself together and come here.' Mom's voice jerked Allison out of her desperation. 'You need to give the police a description of the car, the licence plate, anything you can tell them to help them find Karen.' She was holding the phone out to Allison and then she stood close, her head bent low to the receiver as Allison spoke to the police operator.

'You know this bloke?' Dad looked at Danny. 'You think your sister's in danger?'

Danny nodded. 'She could be. He's pretty rough. Everybody knows what he's like but ...'

'But nobody's ever done anything about it, is that it?' The worry was showing now in the lines on Dad's forehead and in his rapid breathing.

Danny nodded again. 'He's bad – but rich,' he added.

Dad snorted and turned towards Mom and Allison by the phone.

'Maybe I know where he took her,' Danny muttered.

Dad whirled back to face Danny, his head cocked as if he hadn't heard right.

'Maybe I know where she is,' Danny repeated.

Dad looked back at Mom over his shoulder, as if trying to make a decision in next to no time, then he looked at Danny and jerked his head toward the door.

The message was clear. Without saying a word, Danny took his mother's car keys from the hook by the door and the two of them walked quickly out of the house. By the time Mom had hung up they were already backing out of the driveway and no amount of shouting on Mom's or Allison's part reached their ears.

If the scene at Karen's house had taken less than fifteen minutes, Karen's experience of them felt endless. Any time she tried to speak Robbie slapped her, forcing her through the building so that she finally ended up cowering against the back wall of the dirty warehouse, terror gripping her stomach. Through the dusty light filtering down from the broken windows Karen watched Robbie stop and take off his baseball cap while she backed away as far as she could go. When he glanced behind him she realised that two other guys she'd never seen before were in the warehouse with them. Her frantic mind informed her that this made it five to one.

'I tol' you the game wasn't over yet.' Though his voice was soft its tone was sadistic. Still, it was better than him saying nothing at all. For some reason it made Karen feel she still had a chance.

'You didn't have to be so rough.' Karen attempted to sound kittenish, made an effort at a sexy smile, but Robbie lunged at her, arm raised to strike her and she dropped to the floor, scrabbling with her legs to keep away from him.

'Don't give me that stuff no more!' He seemed to tower over her, arm up like a man about to strike a dog.

'Please, please,' Karen began to moan, tears blending with the mucus from her nose. 'Please, don't hurt me.'

'Can it, damn it! Shut up!' His palm came down but instead of hitting her he grabbed a chunk of her hair and yanked her head back so that she was staring into his angry face. His jaw muscles cramped and released, as though he were trying to control himself, and then he let go of her and she slumped back against the wall, pulling her legs beneath her and curling up as tightly as her body allowed.

Robbie stepped back a bit, ran his hand through his

sleek, black hair and chuckled. 'I promised my boys here that I wouldn't hurry. Nobody breathing down our necks here. We'll take it nice and slow. Have a real good time ...'

'Damn right,' somebody said from the shadows.

There was a low, long moaning and Karen was horrified when she realised it was her.

'This here's Drew,' Robbie said, waving off-handedly to his right. 'He's my main man. He gets you first and last.'

'Jackie say he don't want you but he'll hold you down.' Robbie had turned and seemed to be addressing somebody closer to the door.

'Richie – you remember Richie, don'cha?' Robbie was smiling widely now. 'Richie's in charge of the entertainment.'

Karen's stomach churned when she saw Richie raise his right arm and show her the hand-held camera and the zoom lens.

'And Kellogg's our audience.' At this, Karen's stomach heaved and she threw up water and bile onto the floor and the front of her shirt.

'This ain't gonna look too pretty,' Richie said reproachfully, focusing on Karen with the camera.

'Get up.' Robbie's voice was so soft it was almost inaudible but it echoed in Karen's brain and sent her racing heart into a dive. She wanted desperately to comply but her body wouldn't function.

Robbie strode over, reached down and yanked her up.

Karen swayed on her feet. When he took hold of the front of her shirt she opened her mouth to scream but only managed to drool more blood.

Robbie clucked disapprovingly. 'Gotta get her presentable first,' he said as he pulled a bandana from his back pocket and wiped her shirt and her face. 'That's better.' He stepped back to admire his work. 'Kellogg!' he said loudly without turning around.

Kellogg was already coming up behind him. His red hair was shaved close to his head and the freckles across his nose made him look like the friendly neighbourhood paper boy.

'So what do you think of this one?'

Kellogg gave Karen the once over, and shook his head. 'I've seen better,' he said, leering. 'Don't know if this is going to be much of a show.'

Robbie laughed appreciatively, and it was the sound of their merriment, the joshing way they clapped each other's shoulders, that gave Karen a glimmer of strength.

How dare they, she thought suddenly. How dare they frighten me this way, do all this to humiliate me? Allison was right. Robbie was nothing but a bully. A nasty boy who needed to be put in his place. That's why he'd never taken Allison on – he knew she saw through him.

'You won't get away with this,' she said aloud, surprising them all. In the space of a few seconds she seemed like a different person. She was standing tall and straight, and though she was pressed up against the wall her hands were clenched and her face was flushed. 'You can't just do this,' she screamed.

For a second Robbie seemed at a loss for words. It was as if some kind of spell had been broken. A puzzled expression crossed his face and he looked at Kellogg as though hoping he would say something instead. But just as Kellogg opened his mouth there was a crashing noise and as the youths spun around to face the entrance, Karen saw her father and Danny smashing through the doorway.

'Let her go!' Dad's voice boomed in the cavernous warehouse. His fists were clenched by his sides and his slender ribcage was heaving, looking as though it might burst. 'Lay one finger on her and I'll send you all straight down to hell, every one of you!'

Robbie only hesitated an instant, just enough to fully take in who was standing there at the warehouse entrance. 'Dan, my man, who's this old dude?' He had turned his back to Karen and opened his legs wide, hands slightly away from his body, palms open.

'Let her go, Robbie.' Danny's voice was subdued and slightly shaky.

'Come on, now, Danny buddy, we were just going to have some fun. You said it yourself, remember? Sometimes it's just because they ain't never seen a good time and Robbie here's ready to show her one.'

'Daddy,' Karen said, her voice barely a whisper. She

could tell by the rigid line Robbie's muscles were making underneath his shirt that he would not let her pass.

'She's my sister –' Danny started to say, but Dad interrupted him.

'Either you let her go, you piece of slime, or I make you wish you were never born!'

Robbie started to chuckle softly. 'This your Daddy, girl? Fine specimen, I tell ya. Skinny old dude thinking he can chill us, the pride and fury of the Lakeside. Gotta hand it to him, though, all this for some dyke!'

Dad suddenly strode forward, and Robbie's thugs closed in around them. 'This is my daughter.' Dad spoke softly but the tautness of his body, the tremble in the muscles of his arms and along his jawline gave the impression that incredible strength was surging through his slight figure, strength he was trying mightily to contain. 'My flesh and blood. You'll do her no harm.'

Something about the glistening in his eyes, the implication of his willingness to fight to protect her, filled Karen with a sudden strength, a shot of adrenaline that coursed through her limbs and tempered her fear. Stepping quickly forward she moved her foot around Robbie's leg and stomped down hard and swift with the heel of her boot, right onto the tip of Robbie's high-top tennis shoe.

Robbie shrieked, but when he turned to her, slightly bent from the pain, Karen put both hands on his shoulders and shot her knee up straight and true, right between his legs.

Dad seized the moment to release all the trembling energy begging to get out and began lashing out with both fists, landing rapid, cutting punches right, left and centre.

Danny seemed immobilised for an instant, until Richie whipped something out of his pocket and lunged for the pile-up. It was a small, narrow knife. Danny moved then, left the ground in a flying leap that would have allowed him to hit a basket from centre-court and tackled Richie, slamming him down onto the floor and keeping him there with his foot pressed hard on the back of his neck as he tried to decide what to do next.

Dad looked like a cartoon speeded up, punching so fast it was almost a blur. Danny could tell that he was hitting to kill. He was just about to leave Richie and restrain his father for fear of the consequences when a shot was fired behind him. Everybody froze.

'Police! Hands on your heads!'

'Thank goodness, officer,' Danny started to say, going towards them. But the policeman aimed his pistol straight at him and Danny stopped. 'We were trying to save –' he started again, but the policeman interrupted him.

'Everybody against the back wall. Now.'

Danny turned without saying more, seeking out his father and Karen with his eyes. He realised when he caught sight of them that the policeman had no way of knowing the good guys from the bad.

Dad's shirt was ripped, his face bloody, one eye shut

completely. One of his loafers was missing and he was laughing quietly, like a man gone mad. Karen, too, was a wreck, her clothes bloodstained and her face streaked dirt-black and blood-brown. Robbie was limping, moaning with each step. Richie was on the ground, moving slightly back and forth, his hands clutching his chest but making no noise.

'I can explain, officer,' Dad began, hands still on his head, facing the wall.

'That's right,' the policeman said warily. 'You'll all have a lot of explaining to do back at the station.' He and another policeman were frisking them one by one, then handcuffing anybody who looked like he could still move.

'That's my father,' Karen said as the policeman turned her to face him. 'He saved my life.' She looked over at her father, hands cuffed behind him, then up at the policeman beseechingly. He nodded, and Karen ran over and threw her arms around Dad. She kissed his face, though Dad grimaced with every smack that hit his bruised and damaged skin, and put her hand into his, snug in the small of his back. As they walked past Danny, also hand-cuffed, Karen reached out and took his arm. 'And this is my brother.'

'Check inside the car seats,' Karen heard Danny whisper to one of the policemen as they were led to the car. 'Drugs,' Danny answered her questioning gaze when they were safely inside the police car. They started to tell their story on the way to the station, so that by the time they got there the handcuffs were removed and they were taken to the sergeant's office and given hot coffee and cokes.

'Officer Channing gave me a brief rundown,' the sergeant said, leaning back in his chair, 'and that, plus the call from your mother is enough to prove that something very serious happened here.'

Karen nodded, but the strength she had felt was completely drained and she was so weak she could barely hold her cup of cola.

'You'll want to file charges, won't you?'

'I'm afraid,' Karen whispered. 'Maybe next time ...'

'Oh there won't be a next time, dear.' The sergeant looked much more satisfied than Karen felt he had reason to.

'He didn't actually do anything,' Danny interjected, aware of what Karen was thinking. 'We got there first.'

Dad reached over and tousled Danny's hair. 'A fine team, we are,' he said. One side of his face was turning a deep and violent purple, but his good eye twinkled merrily and he seemed deeply pleased with the whole situation.

'Well, there's kidnapping, assault, attempted rape,' the sergeant began, checking the notes on his desk. 'And,' he looked up at them, about to reveal the secret of his happiness, 'enough coke in that car to put them away for a long, long time.'

'Coke?' Dad looked puzzled.

'Cocaine. Your son suggested we rip up that Porsche – and what we didn't find!' He was practically gloating. 'But I need your sworn declarations, and you have to file charges to make sure I can hold him. There's money behind that name.'

Karen looked over at Danny and smiled weakly. 'Okay. What do I have to do?'

It was a long process, interrupted at one point by Mom's arrival. Allison was not with her, but Albert was. The first thing Mom did was practically hurl herself at Karen, tears streaming down her face, and she hugged her so tightly it took Karen's breath away. Still holding on tight to Karen she reached out and took Danny's hand and they sat that way, somewhat uncomfortable, until she released them. Even the sergeant and the police stenographer said nothing to hurry her. She dabbed at Karen's face with a wrinkled piece of tissue pulled out of her purse, wetting it slightly with her tongue the way she used to when Karen was a baby, all the while murmuring how grateful, grateful she was that Karen was all right.

When she looked directly at her ex-husband she almost reached out to try to clean his face as well but something stopped her, and she kept her words and actions to the bare minimum. 'Thank you, Patrick,' she said, putting her hand on his shoulder. Then she turned and went to Albert, who had remained at the doorway. She stood beside him and said nothing more, so the sergeant continued with the report and Karen signed her name to a document that would keep Robbie in jail until he stood trial, and most likely for ten to twenty years after that.

Karen was informed that she would have to testify, and that it would not be easy, but her family spoke up in encouragement and support and she knew she would not be alone. Their unity lasted all the way home, everybody in Albert's car, embellishing on the details until it began to sound like a modern legend.

Mom did not introduce Albert to Dad, and Dad didn't ask who he was, but by the time they walked into the house the mood was breaking and something sombre and sad seemed to be taking over. Albert said a quick goodbye and was out of the house before they'd got their coats off, and the giddy sort of elation that had permeated Dad's demeanour was replaced by heaviness. Mom went into the kitchen to make coffee and they all trailed in after her, knowing that things weren't right but unwilling to face the new feeling alone.

'I'm sorry I caused you trouble, Dad,' Karen said, guilt slipping insidiously into her psyche.

He had stopped at the table but hadn't sat down when she and Danny did, just stood there looking at her, his face too ravaged for her to understand his expression. He shook his head and sighed, and sat down. 'Don't blame yourself.'

Karen wanted more but that was all he said. The ensuing silence was unbearable for her. 'Daddy ... I really ... you saved my life ... you and Danny. Thank you so much for ...'

Dad raised his hand, stopping her mid-sentence. 'Any father would have done the same. Any brother, too.'

The atmosphere around their table was so dense it made Karen feel she wasn't getting enough oxygen. 'You're not mad at me?'

Dad shook his head.

Mom brought the coffee pot to the table, along with four mugs, and poured them each a cup without speaking. She put the pot back on the stove and then sat down in the last chair, looking into her mug rather than at any of them.

'Job's over in ten days, two weeks max,' Dad said suddenly, looking out the window. 'I've got a new assignment. Berlin.'

It was such a total change in direction that Karen wasn't sure she followed him.

'Lake-front hotel,' he added. 'A good six months' work.'

'When are you leaving, Dad?' Danny's voice was so sad, but when Karen glanced over at him his face was blank.

'I move out on the tenth. American Airlines.'

Danny nodded, caught his breath as if he wanted to say something else, but didn't.

'I want you to do something for me, child.' Dad was now looking right into Karen's eyes, using an expression of endearment from his Irish country childhood she hadn't heard since she was little. 'I want you to see a psychiatrist. Any psychiatrist. You choose,' he added hastily, before she could speak. 'I want to hear, when I call, that you are seeing somebody and trying to ... get better.' He reached out and touched Mom's shoulder, making her start and look up from her mug. 'I'll pay for it. Whatever it costs,' he paused, struggling to finish, 'please.'

Karen nodded. She knew she would have agreed to anything he asked at that moment, but there was nothing more. Dad simply finished his coffee, wiped his mouth gingerly on the back of his hand and patted Karen's back as he stood to go.

'I booked a cab for half-past eight, thinking we'd have time to eat together, but no such luck. It's almost that now.'

'You could postpone your departure,' Mom said suddenly, surprising them all. 'I've got all the fixings for a good Irish stew, Patrick, if you've got a mind to have some.'

Dad smiled, looking both puzzled and pleased, but he shook his head. 'Can't. I'm their golden boy. I have to be there tomorrow morning.'

The thought of a hearty, hot stew made Karen's mouth water, though she knew it was also just the idea of it, the warmth and safety it represented right then, that made her want it most. 'Let's make it anyway, Mom, it's fun to cook together.'

Practically giggling like kids about to surprise their parents with a meal, Mom and Karen opened the fridge and began pulling out the ingredients, dividing up the various tasks necessary for their preparation.

Danny was still at the table, watching them. He looked up at his father. 'Maybe I'll just skip the trip to the airport this time, Dad,' he said haltingly. 'I don't really like seeing you off when it's for a long time.'

Dad came over and roughed up Danny's hair. 'Don't tie yourself to your mother's apron strings, son! You don't want to sit here in the kitchen doing women's work, do you? There's nothing a tough Dolan like you can't take, even saying goodbye to his old dad at the airport. Come on. I already paid the cab to take you back.'

He had stretched out his hand, beckoning Danny.

Danny took one last look at his mother and sister, pulling out cutting boards and paring knives, brushing against each other at the counter as they started work, then reached out for his father's hand and stood up. 'I'm just going to the airport with Dad –' Danny started to say to his mother, but she raised her hand, interrupting him.

'Of course, darling, of course! See you later, when the stew's done!' She had turned quickly back to the potatoes so she did not see the fleeting sadness cross Danny's face, nor the tough-boy grin that took its place.

'It's not that I wanted to help in the kitchen,' Danny said to his father as they turned to leave the room. 'It's just that I'm kind of tired, after what we've been through.'

'That's my boy! My fighting partner! Good stuff!' Dad punched Danny's shoulder, making him wince. Then he said goodbye once more to Karen and Mom, and they walked out of the house into the waiting taxi.

11

THREE MONTHS LATER, KAREN STOOD IN HER CAP AND GOWN, her mind wandering while the commencement speakers at her graduation droned on beneath the warm June sun. She could feel its heat penetrating her white gown but the tassel on the graduation cap was positioned in such a way that it kept the direct light out of her eyes, and she could look out at the audience without squinting. So much had happened since her father had left for Germany. The changes were powerful and significant, exemplified by the fact that her entire family was there for this occasion. Things were not perfect, certainly – her mother and Albert were sitting on one side of the stands, and her brother and father were sitting on the other – but at least they were all there, and they planned to go to a restaurant together when the ceremony was over. Allison's parents would not be joining them, and neither would Allison, but Karen felt grateful just the same. She and Allison would have plenty of time to celebrate on their own. They'd been accepted to the same college and got practically giddy at the idea of starting a new life together. Allison had even given Karen a special graduation gift. Karen could feel it pressing against the skin along her chest bone, half a gold heart on a slender gold chain. Allison was wearing the other half.

The college they were going to was known for scholastic excellence. Karen had managed to get a partial scholarship based on her grades and she thought her father would be more exuberant about the news than he had been. He seemed to have trouble bragging about her the way he once did. Still, the psychiatrist he insisted she see turned out to be truly superb. She had made an appointment through her school counsellor and went with the heaviest heart imaginable only to be wholly and joyfully surprised by the psychiatrist's first words, which were that most likely it was the people who asked Karen to go that needed counselling, not Karen. She informed Karen that the psychiatric association had taken homosexuality off its list of mental illnesses and that Karen had, in effect, only one problem – the world at large.

Dr Lawrence was direct and plain in her style, but the sessions made Karen feel stronger and more assured than anything she'd ever experienced in her life. She remembered how eager she had been to tell her father when he first called, and how disappointed she was with his reaction. His first words over the phone were to ask if she'd gone to a psychiatrist. Karen answered in the affirmative, and started to gush enthusiastically about how much Dr Lawrence was helping her, but her father cut her off almost instantly. 'Good, very good,' he said brusquely. 'I'm sure you don't have to go into the details. When are your finals?' He simply hadn't wanted to hear a single word, and the calls after that were the same. Karen didn't need Dr Lawrence to tell her that her father simply couldn't handle the situation any better than that. He'd done his part and he wanted nothing to do with that aspect of Karen's life.

Mom, on the other hand, responded favourably to Dr Lawrence's request that she, too, come in with Karen, and their meetings were emotional, oftentimes, but always helpful. Mom was coming into her own in many ways, not least in her relationship with her daughter. She was realising that she could not shelter her children from the world entirely, nor could she make them what she wanted. She had to simply let them grow up and be who they were, trying to find a way to be a part of the life they led. Mom rose to the challenge and though she was never entirely comfortable with Karen's sexuality, and still could not relax totally when she and Allison were together, she did try very hard to just let her be.

Danny was another story. After Dad had left he withdrew almost totally, spending long periods of time shut away in his room or going out without saying where, dedicating himself more and more to basketball until he practically slept in the gym. Mom responded by attempting to let him know she considered him the man of the house, giving him privileges, like allowing him to stay up late even on school nights, that she was barely ready to grant Karen. Danny continued to be sullen and unresponsive, but Mom attributed it all to a difficult adolescence and put her faith in his ability to work out of it alone. Instinctively, Karen felt it was more than that. There were moments when she'd catch sight of such loneliness on her brother's face she could barely keep herself from running over and hugging him. But the two of them barely spoke, and she didn't dare.

It was Dr Lawrence who'd given Karen an idea for reaching Danny. Once when Karen mentioned to her that Danny seemed happier on the basketball court than any other place, Dr Lawrence suggested that Karen go to see a game. Though Karen was deeply worried she wouldn't be welcome there, and that Danny might give her such a cold shoulder the entire gym would notice, she decided to try it anyway. Dr Lawrence had been right about so many things.

Danny was certainly surprised. He did a double-take when he caught sight of Karen on the bleachers and he did not wave back. Still, she noticed that he'd look her way every time he scored, and he'd acknowledge her thumbs-up sign with a little smile. The first time, Karen left the gym right at the game's end, afraid that Danny might be happy to hug everybody mobbing him except her, but with each game she attended she found him happier to see her there, and it soon got to where he'd look for her anxiously until she showed. Karen promised herself that soon, soon she too would invade the court and throw her arms around him to share his triumph. It was the only real communication they had, her presence at the games and his enthusiastic play-by-play retelling at the breakfast table. It wasn't ideal, but it would have to do for now. For the first time, Karen believed that the future held better things.

Karen was jerked out of her reverie by the realisation that the principal had begun to call their names, one by one, to walk down and accept their diploma. Allison went before she did, and after raising the diploma over her head in triumph she turned slightly to see Karen, and put her hand over her chest, where the half-heart was. Karen responded in kind. People could think what they wanted. Karen was deeply in love with Allison and hoped her future held Allison throughout.

'Karen Dolan.' He had to say it twice before it registered with Karen and she was blushing as she walked down, surprised that she could get so emotional over a simple graduation ceremony. When the principal handed her the diploma, rolled tight and held in a white ribbon, Karen pressed it against her stomach, trying to stall the tears threatening to roll. She had turned to go when she heard, in the general polite applause, whistling and shouts which would have been more appropriate at a sporting event. Karen turned, knowing before she saw them that her father and Danny were on their feet, making a ruckus. Smiling so wide it hurt, Karen raised the diploma into the air and saluted them with it. She caught sight of her mother, dabbing at her eyes with a tissue, but as she walked to her spot Karen no longer felt like crying. She felt like laughing. She didn't know if she'd ever be close to her father. She didn't know if she'd ever share things with her brother. She didn't even know what life would be like now that Albert and her mother were married, but of one thing she was certain. Never again would she deny who she was, not to herself and not to anybody else. The world at large would just have to get used to that.